<u>Books by Jean Rezab</u>

Richmond Sibling Series

Chokecherry Valley Comfort
Chokecherry Valley Joy
Chokecherry Valley Love
Chokecherry Valley Faith

Other Books

In This Place Together
The Prediction

CHOKECHERRY VALLEY FAITH

JEAN REZAB

For Mike, Pat, Theresa, Ron, and Jack

My favorite siblings

ACKNOWLEDGMENTS

Special thanks to the excellent editor, Krista Venero at Mountains Wanted Publishing & Indie Author Services for great suggestions. She helped create a better book than I could have envisioned on my own.

Thank you to the book cover artist at Sunset Rose Books for an amazing cover.

Considerable thanks to my family who have encouraged me in my writing journey.

Thank you to Sally, Ruth, and Amy, great friends who are also great at running book ideas and cover designs past. I couldn't have finished this book without your help.

Special thanks to Connie Victoria Volk for helping by editing and making suggestions for a stronger book. She writes her own books. www.connievolk.com

CHAPTER 1

Alex walked in between the two guards, his cuffed hands in front of him. At least his feet were no longer chained. He took a deep breath, trying to calm his racing heart. Courtney would be waiting. He was equal parts nervous and excited about seeing her again although she visited him only last week.

They reached the waiting area for visitors as they arrived at the prison. The guard asked the desk person for Alex's possessions and took the cuffs off his wrists. The person behind the desk handed him a small manila envelope and a Bible. He reached into the envelope, took out his wallet and stuffed it in his pants pocket, and put his wedding ring on his finger. He'd lost weight in prison, and the ring spun loosely around on his finger.

Sitting around for two years should have made him gain weight, but the lack of interesting food, his poor appetite, and increased anxiety had the opposite effect.

He looked up from his ring, and there stood Courtney. Underneath the red knit hat she wore, she flashed a brilliant smile at him, and he smiled back. It felt almost painful, his facial muscles unused to turning up instead of keeping firmly straight to hide his emotions.

What was she thinking behind her smile? They'd seen each other monthly in the two years he'd been in prison, and she'd stood by him. He suspected there were a lot of things she put up with in Chokecherry Valley she hadn't told him. Just like he kept secrets of what happened in prison from her. They didn't want to waste their time together when they met for the rare visits.

He hadn't wanted her to come more often, even though the prison allowed it. Every time she walked out of the visiting room, he kept himself from begging her to stay. He missed her so much when she left him there to go back to his empty cell.

"You're free to go, Mr. Richmond," the guard said.

"Thank you," Alex responded, keeping to his polite demeanor. He tried to treat the guards politely while in prison. There was no point in being angry at them.

Alex walked over to Courtney, who grabbed him in a tight hug. He held on to her for a bit before pulling away.

"Here's your puffer coat and a pair of gloves. I wasn't sure if you had any winter wear." She handed them to him.

"Perfect." He slid his arm into the sleeve of the black coat and slipped it on the rest of the way.

When he put on the gloves and picked up the Bible, she said, "Let's go."

He caught a glimpse of tears in her eyes as she turned away and walked around the other people waiting their turn at the counter. They reached the outside door. When he stepped outside, the sun shone brightly in the deep blue sky, brilliant and unlike anything he remembered. He blinked and took a deep breath of the frigid December air.

She hugged him quickly again and then let go. "We're over here." She led him to their vehicle, walking carefully on the icy pavement.

He took hesitant steps, as if he hadn't walked on ice for a long time. He kept expecting the prison door to re-open, and the guards to call him back, and put him in his cell again. This freedom was going to take getting used to. He also sensed

Courtney struggling with how to treat him since his release.

"Do you want to drive?" she asked when they reached the vehicle and clicked the door locks open with the key fob.

He automatically headed for the passenger side. He laughed—a rusty, tentative laugh, but a laugh. "I haven't driven for two years. I'll practice when we get home, and there's less traffic. Plus, I haven't looked at my license. I assume it's in my wallet, but it might be out of date."

She nodded, opened the driver's side door, and got in.

The ride out of the exit gate was routine, however when they stopped at the guard's station to leave, Alex had the same fear of being returned to prison. It didn't feel like he was free yet. Everything seemed unreal. How long would it last until the outside world felt like the real world again?

He gripped the armrest every time Courtney took a turn. The closer they got to their house, the tighter he gripped the leather. He should be calmer the closer they got to Chokecherry Valley, but he wasn't sure what kind of reception would greet them. Were there going to be any local reporters or people who resented him for his actions?

Courtney kept glancing over at him.

"What?" he asked.

"You're jittery, aren't you?" Concern laced her voice.

"It's best you know sooner rather than later. I don't sleep well at night. I can't remember the last time I relaxed. I've become afraid of everything. I suppose it was bound to happen."

She didn't tell him it was his own fault because of his confession and consequent prison term. She reached over and touched his gloved hand. "We'll get through it. I'm glad you're home. I'll help you get better."

He relaxed slightly. That was one confession out of the way, and she'd taken it well. Hopefully, they could work through the problems that plagued him, because, being married to him, she had suffered the consequences too.

They reached home. Courtney avoided going through town and took the long way around to arrive behind their house. She parked, and they went in through the back door.

He stood there taking in the scent of home, while Courtney went to look out the windows to see if anyone noticed their arrival. "There's no one out there."

"Good." He walked down the hallway and into the open space of the living room, kitchen, and entryway. During his time away, she hadn't made any changes, and he was grateful for the familiarity of home.

He took off his gloves and his coat and hung them in the entry closet. He sank onto the couch and rested his head against the back. "It's great to be home."

"Do you want something to eat? I made chicken salad and cut up fruit before I left to pick you up. We could have sandwiches with the fruit."

"That sounds wonderful, but you know what I'd really like right now?" He stood up. "I'd like a long hot shower and some other clothes. Do you mind?"

"No, go ahead. I'll get lunch while you enjoy your shower. How about I give you time to get used to your privacy? I didn't move any of your things, so you can find what you need. If you're missing something, let me know."

"I got used to going without." He was glad for time to look around and get reacquainted with the place. He found clothes that might fit, but the pants would probably hang on him. He found a belt for the jeans.

He enjoyed every moment of the shower and felt better when he got into clean clothes. He dropped the ones he wore home from prison into the corner. He might throw them away.

He entered the kitchen in his stockinged feet. "Do you want help?"

"No. I'm fine. It's ready." She pointed to the plates on the table in the kitchen nook. It had a bench seat in the bay window and two chairs around the outer side.

"Good. I'm going to enjoy the great view while we eat." He sat down in one of the chairs, so he could look out the window."

"What would you like to drink?" she asked.

"I'll have water. I'm too jittery for coffee right now."

She got a glass out of the cupboard and filled it with water from the fridge. After she set it in front of him, she got her coffee mug from the counter and joined him at the table.

"I'm glad you're home, Alex. I know relaxing will be hard for you, but other than a few irate neighbors, it's calm around here."

She sounded like she understood, at least. For today, he'd let her wait on him. She wanted to take care of him. But tomorrow, he'd do his share.

She would have to go to work, and he'd somehow have to find work. He'd have plenty of time to provide the meals.

He took a bite of his sandwich, enjoying the taste of something homemade and edible again. He gazed outside, finally feeling a small measure of peace. It would be okay. *Everything will work* out had been his mantra for two long years. Maybe everything would finally be okay.

CHAPTER 2

Courtney found herself second-guessing everything she did. Alex was finally home. She wanted to cry and laugh and scream. Her emotions careened all over the place. On the outside, she tried to look calm. Alex needed that right now.

She was tired of being strong. It had been a long two years without him. She visited monthly, only to leave and come home alone to the house. It felt too big for one person. It was too big for two people.

The house had belonged to Alex's parents until they bought it from them when Alex got his job at the bank. His parents hadn't spent much time here, as they were roaming around the world on one long vacation.

Alex's sister, Ashley, and brother, Paul, approved of them buying the house. Both Ashley and Paul settled in Bismarck shortly after graduation from high school. They hadn't planned to come back to Chokecherry Valley, but now Ashley dated a local guy.

Alex set up guidelines when he went to prison. He refused to see either Paul or Ashley. He also told them not to visit Courtney in Chokecherry Valley. He didn't want his disgrace to rub off on them.

Ashley followed orders until a few months ago. She finally ignored his edicts and paid a surprise visit to Courtney. Ashley said she would support Courtney and Alex now that he was getting out of prison. Courtney could tell Ashley regretted not being around for Courtney sooner, but Courtney had her own family. She had three brothers and two sisters of her own, and her parents were supportive of Courtney and Alex.

She told them if they didn't support Alex too, she wouldn't see them. Her protective family reluctantly said they would treat Alex politely. She hoped they would. They didn't know the whole story, but if they did, they would understand. She hated secrets, but sometimes life forced them on her.

She cleaned up after lunch. There wasn't much to do. Alex settled on the navy-blue cloth couch and stared out the living room window. She could see him from where she tidied the kitchen and wondered what he was thinking. She finished wiping the table and then sat on the chair across from Alex.

His mouth turned up in a smile. "You're staring." He turned to look at her.

"How did you know?" Courtney asked.

His mouth flattened into a grim line. "You learn to read a room by feel when you're around the guys I was around."

She got up and went to sit beside him, taking his hand in hers. "I know this is going to take a while." She waved her free hand around the room. "You've got all the time in the world. I know you're not going to be happy sitting around for long. Have you thought about what you want to do with your time?"

"I'm hoping to get a job but don't have any idea if someone will hire me," Alex said.

Courtney put her arms around him and settled her head on his chest. "We'll work something out. At least we don't need the money."

"The irony of the whole embezzling charge." He slid an arm around her and let out an abrupt laugh.

"There's something I need to talk to you about. Do you want the news now or later?" Courtney asked.

"We may as well talk about whatever it is now. What else do we have to do today besides catch up?"

She nodded. "I know." There was no sense in keeping the news from him. "Steven Hanson is sick again."

He pulled away from her, and she lifted her head to see his expression. She might have to get used to the grim set of his mouth.

He looked down at her. "Same cancer?"

"Same cancer. Only worse this time. They say he might only have a few weeks left. It's metastasized."

"I should go visit him. I'm sure it's been hard on him and Barbara." He stood up and started pacing. "How can I visit them in secret? You know the whole town thinks I shouldn't go anywhere near him."

Courtney watched him. "I know, but he'll want to see you. You know that."

"Yes. I know. We'll have to figure something out."

"He's at home, which makes it easier and harder at the same time. At least they don't live on Main Street like us. Our car would be noticeable if we drove there. It would have been easier if he were in the hospital instead of having hospice at home," Courtney said.

"We'll figure something out." He plopped down on the couch beside her again, and this time, he took her hand. "I'm suddenly very tired."

"Want to go lie down?" she asked.

"No. I'll lean here against the couch. Do you mind staying with me?"

She looked around the living room. Her book was in the bedroom. She'd had a hard time sleeping last night, knowing she would be picking him up this morning. "I'm going to get my book, so if you fall asleep, I'll have something to do."

She got up and headed for the bedroom. It felt good to take a moment to get away from Alex. She didn't quite know how to treat him. Carefully? No. Just as if it were a normal day.

She picked up her book and returned to the living room. "I might fall asleep on your shoulder. It's been a long day, and it's only two o'clock."

She put her book beside her on the couch and settled back in his arms. She wanted to be close to him.

CHAPTER 3

Last night before bed, Alex had delicately told Courtney he needed to sleep alone for a while. He felt hot and flushed when he explained he was fine continuing the physical side of their relationship now, but he couldn't relax enough to sleep with her in the same bed.

He told her about his fear of hurting her in his sleep because he had always been careful to be half aware while in prison. He could lash out if someone touched him when he was asleep.

Courtney looked shocked but then understood. He didn't know what she felt. There were going to be minefields in their marriage until they worked them out.

He'd been gone two whole years. She'd been without him, and he'd been without her. They'd navigated their individual worlds alone. They were more independent and older than they'd been two years ago. They'd made the big decisions together while he was in prison, but the day-to-day problems, they'd negotiated alone.

"Wow," he said as he came into the kitchen and saw the table set in the kitchen nook. He'd heard Courtney get up earlier, but the luxury of staying in a nice soft bed kept him from getting up for a while. He lay there, enjoying the peace and quiet, and the sounds of Courtney in the kitchen. "You made waffles and omelets?"

Courtney smiled at him. "I know. We never ate like this for breakfast, but I thought you might be hungry for real food."

"It smells great. Yes, I am hungry for something not made in a big vat," Alex said.

"I have the whole week off, and I'm going to spoil you," Courtney said. "Have a seat."

Alex hugged her and then sat down at the table. "Okay. Today you can spoil me. Tomorrow we start taking care of each other. I know you didn't have it easy while I was gone. You don't need to pretend."

He saw tears glisten in her eyes before she turned back to the stove. "Okay. We'll take care of each other."

He could barely hear her and knew she fought for control. She dished up the food and delivered it to the table.

"What do you want to drink?" she asked. "There's orange juice, coffee, and water."

"Water. I can get it." He started up from his chair, and she put her hand on his shoulder. He felt her kiss the top of his head.

"I can tell spoiling you isn't going to be easy. I'll get your water, and then we'll do things together."

He breathed out a sigh of relief. "Thanks for understanding, Courtney. I feel guilty for the time you did everything. I want to be helpful."

"I know." She set the glass of water beside his plate and sat down across from him. "And I want to make things up to you for having to endure all you did for the past two years."

They looked at each other across the table, understanding passing between them. Life sucked for each of them in its own way. They had a long way to go for things to be easy between them again, but they'd get there. They'd promised to stick by each other during their marriage ceremony, and he knew Courtney took her vows as seriously as he did.

"Let's make a pact." He placed his hand palm up across the table in front of her, and she put her hand in his. "To many happy days together." He emphasized *together*.

"Together," she said and squeezed his hand. Then she pulled it away.

Her smile said her withdrawal wasn't a rejection. "Let's eat before it gets cold."

His sensible wife. He smiled at her and took a bite of his omelet. It tasted good after all this time. He was suddenly, almost overwhelmingly, happy. "This is terrific."

For the first time in a long time, he felt hungry, and he ate the omelet, two waffles and fruit. He would feel overly full when he was done because his stomach had shrunk, but he enjoyed the fresh meal. When he finished, he settled back in his chair and sipped his water.

Courtney wore a pleased look on her face. She'd been watching him eat. He could feel her eyes on his, but now she concentrated on her own food. She wasn't gulping it down like he had.

She finished up and settled back with her coffee. She must be tired. He had a feeling she hadn't slept well last night or the night before she picked him up.

"Let's make a plan," she said. "First, shopping for new clothes for you."

His heart started to race. "I don't want to be seen around here yet. I'm not ready." He gasped for air.

Courtney slid out of the booth under the window, pulled the other chair up close to him and grabbed his hands. "It's okay. I'm with you. We're not going into Chokecherry Valley."

He nodded, unable to speak.

"We're going to Bismarck. The place is big enough, we shouldn't run into anyone we know from here. We're only going to two places while we're there."

He could feel his heartbeat slowing as she talked.

"We'll go one place to get you clothes that don't fall off you. You only need some pants, underwear, a few belts, and new shoes. Not much. The shirts you have will work okay. They might be a little big for a while, but you'll put on a few pounds eating waffles and omelets every morning." She laughed.

His heart rate returned to normal although his hands tingled from nerves. And from Courtney's touch. Her hands were warm and comforting. He gave her a weak smile. "We are not having waffles and omelets every morning, unless I make them," he said, looking into her eyes.

She had such beautiful blue eyes.

"Hey. Don't go to sleep on me." She tugged on his hands.

"I'm not. I was thinking what beautiful eyes you have." He appreciated the blush rising on her cheeks.

She pulled away as if embarrassed. "Thank you. Now, you seem to be recovered. Let's go shopping. We're going out the back way, and we'll be gone before anyone sees us. The minute our shopping trip becomes too much for you to manage, let me know, and we'll come home."

A few of his nerves returned, but he kept his expression neutral. Eventually Courtney would catch on to what that look meant, but for now, he didn't want to worry her. She didn't know how bad his anxiety had gotten in prison, but she probably already had an idea. He also didn't want it to ruin the day.

"Okay." He put a cheerful note in his voice. "Let's do dishes and get out of here to buy my underwear."

She laughed like he knew she would.

"By the way, you said two stores. What other store do we need to go to?"

"Someplace where they have toiletries. You need a new razor and other things like that. I did pick out things for you but figured you might want to choose other things for yourself."

"Thanks. For everything." He hugged her.

They cleaned up and escaped out the back door. No one saw them leave as far as they knew. They agreed to have a fun day together and not talk about the looming problems they had to address at some point.

CHAPTER 4

Courtney circled around Alex for the next few days. They weren't comfortable living together. She thought, as soon as Alex came home, they would continue their life at ease with each other, even if they had other things happening outside the house.

It wasn't working that way at all. Alex was jumpy and hyper alert. She was unsure of everything he'd gone through in prison. Before he'd been imprisoned, she could have asked him what was going on. Since he'd returned home, she couldn't bridge the distance, almost like a wall separated them.

How long would this go on? She second guessed taking time off from work this week. Maybe it would have been better to let Alex readjust to being home without her.

Their trip to Bismarck to update Alex's wardrobe had been the easiest day so far. They had a common goal. They needed something else to keep them occupied in the next few days.

A light snow of about two inches fell overnight. Not a lot, but enough that it gave Alex something to do outside. He'd been almost giddy at going outside to shovel and sweep the sidewalk and driveway.

A few people drove by on their way to pick up items at the stores on Main Street. Alex pretended not to see them stare avidly out their vehicle windows at him. Word would spread throughout the neighborhood and surrounding area by nighttime that he was out of prison. Which was good. No sense in hiding.

She tidied up the kitchen and heard a vehicle pull into the driveway. She tensed. Who could it be? She didn't get many visitors.

Alex got up from the couch, where he had been reading his Bible, and looked out the window. "It's Paul and Ashley."

Courtney's mouth stretched into the first natural smile since Alex returned home, and her shoulders relaxed about four inches. "Ashley stopped by a few times in the past few months. I forgot to tell you."

Alex frowned. "We told her to stay away."

"We did," Courtney said as she headed for the front door. "Your sister has developed quite a backbone in the past six months. She refused to leave one day, so I finally let her in."

"I don't like it. They're not supposed to be involved." He continued frowning.

"You tell them then." She gestured toward the door.

He didn't move from his spot by the couch.

She opened the door. "Hi, Ashley."

Ashley swept her into a hug. "Hi. I brought Paul with me."

"I see. Hi, Paul."

"Hi," he said.

Courtney ushered them into the house. Ashley slid off her sneakers, which were wet from the snow. Paul tugged off his shoes too.

Courtney noticed Alex stood there staring at them from his place in front of the couch. She took their coats and hung them in the closet by the door.

They all looked at Alex, who finally spoke. "I told you—"

Ashley ran over to him before he could finish and pulled him into a tight embrace. Courtney could almost feel the rigidity of his frame from her place by Paul.

Alex finally lifted his arms and encircled Ashley in a big hug. Courtney let out the breath she'd been holding.

When Ashley and Alex let go, Ashley looked him in the face. "I know what you said. Well, that doesn't matter anymore. You're where I can see you, and you need company. You're not going to hide out in shame from your own family. Whatever happened is in the past. I left Courtney alone for too long, but that's over. You're stuck with Paul and me now. Get used to it."

Alex looked at her as if he'd never seen her before.

"You look surprised I'm not the doormat I used to be." Ashley grinned at him.

Alex looked over at Paul, who shrugged. "What can I say? She's got me talked into visiting you. I see her point."

"But what about your reputations?" Alex sounded doubtful.

"Who cares?" Ashley asked. "Paul's job is in Bismarck. They don't care. I'm in school. No one there cares either. We don't work here in Chokecherry Valley. Besides, you did the time. They better start getting over it."

Alex shrugged helplessly. "Well, it's complicated."

Paul came over and sat on one of the chairs across from the couch. "We always knew that. But you didn't tell us then, and you're not going to tell us now. So, I guess we'll pretend it's not complicated and love you anyway."

Courtney saw a shimmer of tears before Alex blinked and sat down on the couch.

"Okay. I guess I'm stuck with you." A big smile broke out on his face as he looked around the room.

Courtney relaxed even more. Finally, she had someone else to share the load. Reintegrating Alex into the neighborhood would be hard enough with his anxiety and the community's anger.

Paul settled back on his chair and stuck his black stockinged feet out in front of him. "You may as well know right away I have news. I got engaged last month. Her name is Hannah."

Alex got up and shook his hand before settling back on the couch. "That's great. Where did you meet her?"

"She works at the hospital too. She does fundraising, and I was involved in one of her fundraisers. We got to know each other, and now, here we are.”

“I saw a picture of you online. You gave that kid a scholarship, which was nice of you to do.”

Paul’s face flushed bright red. “Yes. It was the least I could do for him, but the story is for another time.”

Alex turned to Ashley. “How about you, Squirt? Or maybe I should change your nickname to Feisty.”

Ashley laughed and sat down on the other cushioned chair beside Paul’s seat. “If you want something, you have to go after it.” She glanced at Courtney.

Courtney smiled at her and joined Alex on the couch. “Like you did to me. Camping on the front porch until I let you in.”

“I’d had enough of the separation,” Ashley said. “Besides, it was time to get this family back together.”

“And what about the other person you come to see in Chokecherry Valley?” Courtney asked slyly.

“Oh, him.” Ashley shrugged like it was no big deal.

Alex leaned toward her now. "Out with it. Who is this guy?"

Now Ashley's face turned red. "It's Jason. You know? The guy who lives by Paul's in-laws."

"You mean Jason Allmen?" Alex asked.

"That's him," Courtney said gleefully.

Ashley threw her a quick smile. "Okay. You've had your fun." She turned back to Alex. "So far we've been on one date, and he came to my apartment for a few hours Thanksgiving evening."

"And they have lunch after class a lot of times," Courtney added.

"That's where you met him? In class?" Alex asked.

"Yes. We were sitting beside each other, and things kind of happened. I never dreamt I'd seen him before, but I must have."

"You stayed with Grandma in Bismarck a lot of times and went to high school there. If you'd been here when you were that age, you probably would remember him," Paul said.

"Probably." Ashley shrugged and smiled. "I guess I've met him now."

Courtney suddenly jumped up from where she'd been sitting. "I'm sorry. I didn't even offer you anything to eat or drink. Can I get you something?”

Ashley and Paul both shook their heads.

“We’re fine. We snacked on licorice and mixed nuts on the way here,” Ashley said.

“You mean, you did,” Paul teased her, then shook his head at Alex and Courtney. “She’s kind of going through a licorice phase right now.”

Ashley laughed but didn’t argue.

Alex continued smiling, but Courtney could sense strain behind his smile now. She wasn’t sure why. She couldn’t read his moods like she used to. She almost sighed before realizing that wouldn’t be the best thing to do around company. Even if the company was Alex’s family. And hers.

She knew it was time for them to leave. Alex wasn’t used to long social visits.

Paul leaned forward and clasped his hands between his knees. “Just so we’re clear. Ashley and I will continue to visit. Sometimes together. Sometimes alone. Sometimes with Hannah or Jason, but you’re not in prison anymore, and you’re not alone anymore.”

Alex lifted his hand to stop him.

“Don’t worry. I’m not going to get all mushy on you. I just needed to say that. I couldn’t get to you in prison because you could refuse." He looked Alex in the eyes. "Which is the only reason you didn't see me."

He leaned back again and looked up at Courtney, who hadn't sat down after her offer of refreshments. "And I shouldn't have listened to you. I'm glad Ashley forced her way back into your life, but we should have done it sooner, Ashley and I agree."

He looked uncomfortable then. "Of course, my life was in a bit of a mess there for a while. Maybe it's for the best." He stood up and walked over to Courtney.

"Can I give you a brotherly hug?" he asked.

"Of course." She hugged him back.

"I'm sorry we weren't here for you. Next time we visit, we'll keep the conversation light."

She smiled at him. "Sounds good."

Paul looked at Ashley. "We should head back and let these two have some privacy."

Ashley hugged Alex and Courtney when they stood up from the couch. "Okay, but we'll be back."

After they had their shoes and coats back on and were walking down the driveway, Alex yelled out the door at them, "And next time, bring a Christmas present."

He laughed at their twin expressions of surprise. And then they were grinning and waving back at him. He laughed and closed the front door.

Courtney stared at him, her mouth open. "Wow. Where'd that come from?"

"I finally realized I'm actually home. And it's December. And it's almost Christmas." He grinned at her and pulled her into a tight hug.

She relaxed into the hug and laid her head on his shoulder. Maybe everything would be okay. She pushed all thoughts away about all the steps necessary to a normal life. It could wait. Maybe if they concentrated on Christmas and took everything else as it came, it would work out.

CHAPTER 5

Alex woke up Monday morning when he heard the shower start. Courtney was getting ready to go to work. Their brief time alone was over, and he knew he needed to visit Barbara and Steven. He'd given him the job at the bank when Alex graduated from college. While he didn't owe him anything, he needed to see him before the cancer progressed any further, and it was too late to talk to him.

When Courtney returned from church yesterday, she gave Alex the update that Steven only had weeks to live. Alex knew there wasn't much time, but now that he was out of prison, he could act.

Courtney came into the bedroom wrapped in a bath towel to get her clothes from the closet. She took up residence in one of the guest rooms until they were comfortable with each other again. She told him to take his time, and he knew the decision was in his control. She was ready to be a married couple any time he said the word. He wondered how patient she would be.

She pulled clothes out of the closet and turned to look at him where he lay on the bed. "What are you doing today?"

"Going over to see Steven and Barbara. I think it would give him some peace."

"You're a nice man, Alex Richmond." Her words came out softly as she struggled to juggle her clothes and her towel.

He ducked his head. He wasn't used to good things being said about him. "Thank you. What time are you done with work?" He looked back up at her.

"Around 2:30 p.m."

"I'll be here waiting. We can take a walk before it gets dark outside. It's in the thirties today, and we won't have very many more days this warm."

"Sure. Sounds good. I'm going to grab a banana on my way to work, so you're on your own for breakfast." She left to dress and get to work.

He lay there a few more minutes before deciding he should get moving himself. From now on, he'd make breakfast for Courtney. She was the only one currently working, and his choice of job was limited by his stint in prison. It could take a long time before someone would hire him.

The idea didn't depress him as much as he believed it would. He didn't want to hang around for a long time with nothing to do, but the visit from Paul and Ashley lit a fire in him to make a great Christmas for them all.

He would check with Courtney when they took their walk and ask if she was willing to host his family and their significant others for Christmas Eve or Christmas Day.

She'd been understanding yesterday about church. He wanted to go, but if they did it in stages, it might be more manageable for Courtney. First, everyone would know he was out of prison. Next week when he attended church with her family, the initial gossip would have died down. He hoped.

And her family's response to his attendance would be intense. He knew they'd be polite to him in front of Courtney, but how would they treat him when she wasn't around? He had no idea.

Courtney's family went to church in Bismarck, so at least it wasn't the local Chokecherry Valley church. He had nothing against the church. In fact, he wanted to stop there and visit with the local pastor in the next few days. He was glad Courtney didn't have to put up with everyone's stares. But he was wrong. She'd already done that by working at the local grocery store.

He felt ashamed. She put up with the local animosity while he'd been in prison. How did she stand it? Her firm conviction everything would work out okay got her through the days. He hadn't wanted to suggest they sell the house and move where nobody knew them.

He'd plan one last Christmas in this house where he'd grown up, and then, in the new year, they could start fresh. They had the money. At least there was no problem with that aspect. He wanted to contribute something to society since he'd been given a lot from his parents, and they had a beautiful house and food to eat.

He called Barbara, who answered with a delighted laugh. "I'm glad you're home," she said. "I've been waiting to hear from you."

"Thank you, Barbara. Courtney and I were trying to get a few things settled, but she's at work today. I was wondering what a suitable time would be to visit you and Steven."

"Anytime. Really. He sleeps a lot when he's not in pain. A visit from you might settle him down.

He's asked about you a few times." There was a sudden catch in her voice.

"I know," he said softly. He'd lost one of his good friends to cancer in college and never got over seeing the results of the disease, especially at the end of Kevin's life. "I'll be over in about a half hour. I'll come the back way to keep gossip to a minimum. Hopefully, I'll be in and out before anyone passes on the news I'm visiting."

"Oh, Alex." Her voice held a note of sorrow. "It shouldn't be this way."

He took a deep breath. "I'm fine, Barbara. I'll be over soon. Don't worry. Things worked out for the best. I'll tell you all about it someday."

"Thanks, Alex. You're a good man."

"See you soon." He hung up and laughed. Well, two women in one day thought he was a good man.

He didn't know where he fell on the scale of goodness. Two years of being locked up and keeping to himself stunted his ability to look at people normally. He'd always been assessing the other prisoners for threats although a lot of them were as scared as he was. They had to keep up an attitude in prison to survive. He saw beneath the surface to the good in some of them who had been caught in circumstances and made poor choices.

He looked around the kitchen and living room, wondering what to do with himself for the next thirty minutes. Most of the time since he'd gotten out of prison, he felt like he was looking at himself from an outside lens. He wasn't comfortable anywhere anymore. His cell had been his peaceful place.

He finally got out the Bible he'd brought with him from prison. He sank down on the couch and held it in his hands without opening it. Just holding it grounded him somehow. He finally opened it to his favorite verse about God's peace surpassing all understanding and felt his shoulders relax as he read.

Twenty minutes later, his emotions under control, he put on his shoes and coat. He found the leather gloves Courtney insisted he buy and smiled. She'd convinced him to buy more than he intended that day, but they had fun. He had a feeling he'd need everything she thought he did.

He left through the rear door. He liked the slight cold breeze ruffling his dark hair as he took the back path to Steven and Barbara's house. There was only one house between them, and he hoped they weren't looking out their back window as he walked along the gravel road. It was for their sake, not his. He could handle it. He and Courtney agreed, if she heard anything he needed to know, she would text him from work.

He walked up to the Hansons' back door, which Barbara opened before he reached it.

"Hi." She gave him a tight hug, then released him, and took a long look at him. Something in his expression must have convinced her things were okay between them. She relaxed. "It's good to see you."

"You too." He smiled at her, removed his gloves, and took her hand in his. "I'm sorry."

Her smile faltered, and tears filled her eyes. "We hoped when he was in remission, it wouldn't return, but here we are."

This time he pulled her into a hug. She rested against him and then pulled away, wiped her tears with her hand, and pulled out a tissue to wipe her nose. "A word of warning. He's lost a lot of weight."

Alex nodded and followed her into the house. They were in the back hallway that led past the bedrooms and into the main living room. Steven's bed was close to the wall. He could look outside the front windows or turn his head to the other wall and see the fireplace.

Alex stuffed his gloves into his pockets and unzipped his coat, slipping it off as he walked over to the bed. This was not the six-foot husky man Alex had seen two years ago. His face was sunken, and his hands clenched the sheets. His eyes burned into Alex's as Alex approached the bed. Barbara disappeared into one of the other rooms to give them privacy.

"Hey there," Alex said.

"Hi." His voice was low but still held a hint of strength running through it. "Good to see you. I've been pestering Barbara to see when you were coming." He smiled in the direction his wife had gone. "She told me to be patient."

"Patience is not your main virtue," Alex kidded him.

He sighed. "Well, I've gotten better at it since I got sick. Can't do much more than wait now."

"Sorry it came back."

"I know you are, but you gave me everything you have, and I won't forget. Barbara won't forget either when I'm gone," he said.

"There's nothing that can be done? No more treatment options?" Alex asked.

"Nothing. I'm resigned and ready to go. I've had two more years with Barbara than I expected. I'm lucky. I've led a good life with only a few poor choices—one big one I pray both you and God forgive." He turned his head away and coughed.

It hurt Alex just listening to him. It was painful to see his friend and mentor lying there helpless.

When the coughing fit passed, and he turned back around, Alex said, "I've forgiven you, and if you've asked God for forgiveness, I know He's forgiven you too. I'm moving on with my life." He frowned. "Well, that was a poor choice of words."

Steven laughed, which made him cough again. "And I'm done moving."

"I am sorry." Alex wished there were a way out of this, but nothing would change the outcome.

"You have nothing to be sorry for. I'm the one who's sorry."

"It's over. Let's talk about something else."

"The kids have been here. Mary's finished with college, and Sarah graduates next year. I can't believe they're grown and going to start their lives already."

Alex wondered what Barbara was going to do when both girls were gone and Steven too. He'd have to figure out what he could do to help her. "That's great. They're both doing terrific, from what I've heard."

He smiled like the proud father he was. "I think so."

Barbara came into the room. "Do either of you need anything?"

Alex shook his head. "I'm fine."

Steven reached out his hand to Barbara, and she held it lightly. "Thank you for getting Alex over here."

"Oh, he called right away this morning." Barbara smiled fondly at Alex.

"Yes, you're my first stop, although my brother and sister came by on Saturday to visit. Courtney finally felt she could stop babysitting me yesterday and went to church with her family." He grinned at Steven. "Things are going quite well. Nothing to worry about, so you rest."

He turned to Barbara. "And you get some rest too. I'm only a short distance away. Feel free to call me any time you need something."

Alex pulled his cell out of his jacket pocket and asked Barbara what her number was. She gave it to him, and he punched in the numbers and called her. They could hear her phone ringing on the kitchen table. Alex hung up. "There. You have my number."

"Wow," Barbara laughed, "you didn't waste any time getting connected."

Alex shook his head. "That's Courtney. She had the phone ready for me from the moment I left the prison."

Steven winced at the word "prison," and Alex realized that wasn't a good topic. "I'm going to pay her back by texting her constantly." He smiled at them both.

"Somehow I don't believe she'll mind," Barbara said.

Alex reached for his coat, which he'd thrown on the chair when he came into the room. "I know this has been brief, but you need your rest, and I'll be by frequently."

"You come by anytime you want," Barbara said.

Steven nodded his agreement.

"The community might not be happy I'm visiting you." Alex knew he had to broach the subject.

"We don't care. I won't be here much longer," Steven said. "I prefer you to visit when you want. Those who complain don't matter."

Alex caught the pain in Barbara's eyes when Steven said he didn't have much longer. "Okay. I'll be back." He patted his hand, but before he could withdraw his own hand, Steven turned his over. With a strength Alex hadn't expected, he gripped Alex's hand.

"Thank you. I'll pay you back." He squeezed Alex's hand and then let go, his eyes burning into Alex's.

Alex nodded and followed Barbara to the back door.

"Thank you for giving him time," Barbara said. "He wanted to tell you he was sorry."

"I know. It's okay." He wanted to get out of there now. He was starting to feel the claustrophobia he'd felt when he first entered prison and knew he couldn't leave whenever he wanted.

He waved at Barbara, who watched him walk down the drive. Then he was out of her sight and took a deep breath of the fresh air. He didn't walk directly back to his house. There was a side path that didn't lead anywhere but toward some pastures. He wandered along it.

There'd probably been about four inches of snow covering the ground from previous snowfalls. Soon his shoes were full of snow, and he headed back home. He was going to have to find boots to wear if he was going to take walks off the cleared paths.

He thought about his visit with Steven, and he remembered how he'd looked when Alex went to prison. The chemo took a toll the first time, and he retired from the bank the day Alex pled guilty to embezzlement. Steven said he wanted to spend any time he had left with Barbara. They had all been happy when he'd been declared cancer-free six months later.

Then, a year later, the cancer returned. They fought against it for six months now, and from what he'd heard today, they'd reached the end of options. Alex shook his head. At least they had the past two years, even though some of the time had been fighting his illness. Alex was sure it didn't feel like enough time to them. He knew, if Courtney were sick, he would do anything to spend the end with her.

He texted Courtney to ask her when she'd be home for lunch. He was determined to make her lunch today and have something waiting for her when she got home.

He was looking through the cupboards and fridge to see what he could make when he heard the doorbell. The sudden sound made him jump. He couldn't imagine who was visiting, and did they want to see him? Or had they come to see Courtney?

He walked over to the door and opened it to see Mary Hanson standing on the front welcome mat.

"Hi," he smiled in welcome, "do you want to come in?"

He noticed she didn't smile back. In fact, her face set in a fierce frown.

"What are you doing?" she asked, ignoring his invitation to enter.

He was confused by her manner and tone. He always thought they were friends, even though five years separated them. He'd spent so much time at her parents' house, he felt like Mary and Sarah were like sisters to him. "What do you mean, what am I doing?"

"Visiting my dad like that."

His own lips turned downward at her words. "Of course I visited him and your mom. They

wanted me to come over and see them. Were they
upset I was there?" He was surprised that he
misread the situation.

Mary stomped her foot on the mat. "No,
they weren't upset. I'm upset. You need to stay
away from them. You're not doing them any good
by going over there."

"What do you mean? They were happy to
see me," he repeated.

"Of course they were. They love you. But
this is a small town. What happens when word gets
around you were over there? They're going to be
gossiping about my parents. They don't need that
right now." Mary looked at him like he had the
understanding of a kindergartner.

"Now I'm back in town, people are going to
talk no matter what I do."

"Maybe you should leave town until my
father dies then," she suggested with a hint of tears
in her eyes. "This relapse is all your fault anyway.
He was getting better. He was in remission, and
then he started thinking about you coming back to
Chokecherry Valley, and the cancer returned."

Alex looked at her for a long moment. He
didn't quite know what to say to her charge. In fact,
there was nothing he could say. The one thing he

knew was Steven's impending death wasn't his fault, and Courtney knew it too.

However, other people in Chokecherry Valley would see things the same way Mary did. Without Steven disputing the allegation, that was the way it had to be. There was no way Alex was bringing him into this mess when he only had a few weeks to live.

"I'm sorry, Mary. I don't like hurting you, but your father and mother are more important right now. They want to see me. Until they tell me to quit coming over there, I need to respect their wishes." He held up his hand to stop her because he could see she was going to continue the argument.

"I don't want to hurt you. You've been hurt enough. If you talk to your parents about your feelings, please be gentle. If they don't want to see me, I'll stay away."

She turned away without another word and walked down the front steps and back down the street.

He closed the front door and went back to his perusal of the kitchen. Courtney would be home soon. As he made lunch, he pondered Mary's visit. What a mess. Maybe two years ago he and

Courtney made the wrong choice. At the time, it seemed the right thing to do.

He pushed the thoughts away and smiled at Courtney as she came in the front door. He set two plates on the island. "Lunch is served."

She took off her boots on the entry rug and pulled off her coat and scarf before hanging them on the closet door by the entry. "Sounds good, whatever it is. It's nice to have someone cook."

He laughed. "Well, I didn't exactly cook. It's just a few turkey and cheese sandwiches, and I mixed up a simple lettuce salad."

"Good enough. I'm starving. We were busy at the grocery store today. People are already getting ready for Christmas baking. Butter, flour, and chocolate have been flying off the shelves." She sat on one of the counter stools.

"What do you want to drink?" he asked.

"Water." She took a big bite of the sandwich. "Yum. You put salad dressing on it."

He set a glass of ice water in front of her. "I tried to remember how you liked it."

"This is perfect." She helped herself to salad and poured French dressing on it.

Alex joined her at the island, sitting on the stool next to her, and started eating his own sandwich. He tried to decide if he should tell her about Mary's visit or wait until Courtney finished work for the day. Putting it off was probably the wrong way to go. Courtney might run into Mary yet today, and it wouldn't be fair to not warn her.

She happily ate her way through her food. He enjoyed her appetite and pleasure in the simple meal. He'd try and give her something warm in the coming days since the weather was turning colder. He'd make a list and go shopping.

"There are a few things we need to talk about." He set the rest of his sandwich on his plate. He'd deliberately waited for her to finish her sandwich, and she was almost done with her salad.

Her fork clattered to her plate, and she twisted around on her stool to look at him. "You sound serious."

He saw the fear in her eyes and hurried to dispel whatever caused that expression. "One subject is shopping." He smiled, "Relax and finish your salad."

She gave him a tentative curve of the lips and went back to eating.

He noticed she wasn't eating as heartily as before. Why did this have to be complicated? "I want to pick up groceries so I can make you hot meals to eat. You know? Casseroles, soup, lasagna…"

She put down her fork and pushed her plate away. She almost managed to finish the salad. She turned again to look at him. "Lasagna. My favorite."

"Homemade lasagna."

Her smile spread into a big grin. "You don't know how to cook. I used to do all that."

He was relieved to see the grin on her face. "You used to cook. I'm going to learn now."

She groaned, although the smile remained. "I'm going to be the guinea pig, aren't I?"

"Well," he paused, "I guess you could put it that way."

"I'm in," she said, sliding off the stool. "If you're going to cook, I'll try it all. I'm not saying I'll eat a full helping of everything, but I'll make the attempt."

He laughed. "Fair enough. My question is, do you want me to come to your workplace to get groceries, or would you rather I go to a neighboring town to buy the food? It doesn't matter to me."

She didn't hesitate. "You may as well come to the store where I work. We live on Main Street and can't hide away. My boss is supportive of me and won't care. I refuse to run away and hide."

"Okay." He stood up and gave her a gentle hug. "I'll shop there tomorrow."

She hugged him back. "I guess I need to get back to work. This was nice." She started toward the entryway to get her boots and coat.

He might as well rip off the Band-Aid. "One more thing. Mary came over and was upset I'd gone over there to visit this morning."

She paused in the act of putting the scarf around her neck. "Why was she upset?"

"She blames me for her dad's cancer coming back. Said he was in remission, and the thought of me getting out of prison caused him to get sick again."

She shook her head. "You know that's not true."

"Yeah, I do, but there's no easy answer. Steven and Barbara want to see me. Mary doesn't want me to go over there. This is getting complicated."

Courtney stared at him from her place on the entry rug. He walked over and gave her another hug. "Sorry. I needed to warn you."

She returned his hug again. "Hey. We knew this was going to get difficult. Thanks for the warning. Don't spend time worrying about it. Make up the grocery list. I'm looking forward to seeing what you make." She turned and opened the door.

He thought she would just leave but was surprised when she turned around and looked directly into his eyes. "I love you—don't forget. And put canned soup on the list so when you have cooking disasters, we can eat soup."

She laughed and closed the door on him. He knew his mouth was hanging open for a good five seconds before he shut it and laughed. That was Courtney. A good sense of humor when it was needed. In one sentence, she'd released a lot of his own worry over how this was affecting her. Obviously, she'd had two years of practice while he was gone.

He gave God thanks for being available for Courtney. He knew Courtney's family had also been supportive of her. He was going to have to face them eventually. Later.

CHAPTER 6

Alex got out a few recipe books from the drawer in the kitchen. His first foray into cooking would be learning to make lasagna. He wrote out the ingredients on a shopping list and added other items he missed eating while in prison. Realizing he hadn't asked Courtney what she wanted, he wrote a few items she liked in the past. He'd ask her on their afternoon walk to add any other food she wanted to the list.

When she got home, they took a pleasant walk. He told Courtney he was going to visit Steven again in the morning, and then he would stop at the store for the groceries he'd put on the list.

"I'll start looking around for a job in the afternoon," he said.

"Oh, there's no hurry." Courtney looked up with wide, startled eyes. "You just got home."

"I can't sit around doing nothing while you're out working. That isn't fair."

"You know I started working to have something to do while you were gone."

"You can quit if you want." He wasn't sure if she wanted to continue working or not.

She was silent for a while. "I'm not sure I want to quit. It's an easy job. My boss is nice. It gives me something to do."

"I can understand. I don't want to sit around either. There are too many memories I don't want to dwell on anymore. The past is in the past. I want to look forward to the future. I'm considering going back to college."

Again, there was a pause before Courtney responded, "I think it's great you want to go back to school, but you need to know. Finances are beginning to be an issue."

He stopped in the middle of the road where they were walking. The chill in the air spread throughout his body. What new problem was this? He wasn't sure he wanted to hear it, but there was no sense in avoiding the subject.

Courtney looked down at the ground. She didn't appear to want to talk about it either. Obviously, since he'd been home for days, and she hadn't brought it up.

"Let's go home and talk about this over some hot chocolate," he said.

She looked up at him and took the gloved hand he held out. They silently trod along the snow-covered ground.

He was busy wondering about the finances, but he had no idea what she was thinking.

They settled on the couch with the hot chocolate on the coffee table in front of them.

"Okay. I'm ready." He gave her a big smile. "We'll figure it out together."

She smiled. "It's nice to hear the word 'together.'"

"I realize you managed everything while I was gone. We need to start communicating about everything again," he said and felt her stiffen beside him.

"That sounds like a tall order." She withdrew to the other end of the couch and pulled her feet up in front of her, winding her arms around her knees. "We don't have enough money for you to go back to school," she said bluntly. "I did what I could, but the money went fast in the last few years.

"There was the help we gave to Steven and Barbara. That was a chunk. I've been living here and fixing things up as cheaply as I could without cutting corners. The heating bill, groceries, and other things have all gone up in price. The gas I used to go see my family. We remodeled the kitchen just before you went to prison. That took another big outlay, but we weren't concerned. You were still working, but we haven't had your income since then."

"It can't be that bad," Alex said.

"When are you going back to work?" For the first time since he got out of prison, he heard hostility in her voice.

"I don't know," he said, puzzled.

"I know you don't know. I don't know either. That's my point. We're only in our late twenties. We've got years to live. I'll go over the accounts with you tomorrow and show you what we have. If you go back to school, we will use up what we're living on now. There won't be a lot of room for error. We'd be giving up our cushion. You need to find work before you decide to go back to school."

"How many other things are wrong you haven't told me?" He was starting to see she was used to taking responsibility for everything, and he'd let her. When she'd visited him, she hadn't told him anything about her home life, except the good stuff. And he hadn't asked questions either. He assumed since she hadn't brought up any problems, she wasn't having any.

"Did you see the egg stains on the siding on the front of the house? That happened this week," Courtney said.

"I didn't notice." He couldn't believe he missed the mess, but he scurried out of the house to hide from anyone whenever he left. He didn't stick around to inspect the outside of their home.

"You've been coming in the back door. They don't do anything back there. They want others to see what they've done."

"Do they leave you alone at work?" He was suddenly worried about her. Two years too late, he decided.

"Yes, my boss made it clear from the beginning if they treated me badly, they weren't welcome in her store, and a lot of them pretend I'm not there. But there are others who are kind and take the time to talk to me and ask me how I'm doing." She sniffled.

He reached toward her, and she moved to cuddle in his arms. "I'm sorry. You always seemed strong when you talked about what's happening," he said.

"There was nothing you could do. My sisters came and spent time with me, and we'd have little parties when they sensed I was getting down. They were good for me."

Thank goodness she had a big family who took care of her.

"From now on, let's talk about these things. I could clean the egg off the front siding tomorrow."

"People will see you," Courtney objected.

"When was the last time someone egged the house?"

"Not since right before you came home," she said.

"Word is out, and the community knows I'm home. There's no reason to hide anymore. My first official outing will be going to the grocery store tomorrow.

"I'll be seeing Steven and Barbara, but I'll still go the back way. Mary's already upset, so I hope we can keep those visits a secret at least. I guess the rest of people's responses we'll have to deal with as they happen."

"I guess," Courtney said.

"And school is out of the question for now. As a convicted felon, I don't know what's going to happen. We'll look at finances tomorrow and see

what needs to be done. I do have a business degree.
I should be able to set up some kind of budget."

"I've already done that." Her voice was
sharp again.

He hugged her closer. "Sorry. Of course you
have. We'll look at it together. I can get the full
picture, and we'll see what kind of job an ex-
convict can get."

She patted his leg. "Don't undersell yourself
and don't use the word 'ex-convict' in front of me
again. We both know what happened. You're a
good guy. Don't forget what you did for your
friends."

"I'll try. But you paid as big of a price as I
did by helping them. Don't forget I know that too."

CHAPTER 7

Courtney walked to work the next morning in the bitter chilly air. The thermometer on the side of the house registered ten degrees outside. She wore a hat and wrapped a scarf around her lower face and neck. The wind stung her eyes. She was glad the store was only a block from her home.

She walked into the store and greeted Betty, "Good morning. How are you?"

Betty stood at the till, checking the bills and change in the drawer. "I'm good. It's a cold one out there, but at least it's not snowing. How are you and Alex doing?"

"Oh, you know. One step forward, one step back. Someday we'll get to two steps forward and one back."

She considered Betty a friend. Betty gave her a job and defended her decision to hire Courtney when people complained. She'd stood firm in her support, and Courtney appreciated it. Except for her family and Barbara, Betty was one of the few people who treated her kindly. Although some ignored her she preferred that to the sneering stares of others.

"He'll come around, and you'll get used to being together again. It takes adjustment time." Betty's plump cheeks were still rosy from the chill outside. Beneath her lovely white hair, her eyes were kind and understanding.

Courtney held back the tears. "Thank you. I'm going to get those shelves stocked from those boxes that came in yesterday." She hurried to the back of the store.

"Thanks, dear," Betty called after her retreating back.

Courtney took a few deep breaths, wiped her eyes, and concentrated on work. At least here, she was usually busy enough to put aside thoughts of her current relationship with Alex. They would work things out. She knew that. But it was still hard getting through this phase. She'd believed, once he was home, everything would go back to the way it had been before he left.

She started putting cans of various vegetables on the shelves, listening to Betty's soft voice whenever a customer came in and visited with her. It was getting close to lunchtime when she heard a familiar male voice.

"Hi, Betty," Alex said.

"Alex! It's good to see you." Courtney peeked around the corner of the shelf she finished stocking. She saw Betty walk over to Alex and give him a hug. "You've lost weight, but those eyes still have a lot of sparkle in them."

"Are you flirting with me?" Alex hugged her back.

"Not with that wife of yours working for me. She's a hard worker, and I don't want to lose her. Besides, you know me—no shenanigans."

Courtney started toward the front of the store. "Betty is immune to your charm."

Alex's smile widened as he saw her. "Thank goodness I have you then."

"Don't you forget." She smiled back. "Are you here to do the grocery shopping?"

"Yep." He put his gloves in his pocket and pulled out the list he had started the day before. "Anything specific you want before I start?"

She reached out for the list and looked it over. "This looks like an ambitious list. I'd add mint chocolate chip ice cream. No specific brand." She handed the list back to him.

"I'll get right on that," he said.

She watched him pull out a cart and start down one of the aisles.

"At least you're training him right from the start." Betty smiled. "Get the groceries."

"He said he wants to cook. I'll have him start doing laundry next week."

"I heard you," Alex called over his shoulder.

She and Betty laughed together.

Courtney returned to finish stocking the last shelf, then moved the empty boxes to the back room. The stockroom was full of empty boxes, and she just finished when she heard yelling out in the store. She rushed out to help Betty with the situation.

Van Hanson stood in front of Alex's cart. "You don't belong here. You should still be in prison. It's because of you Steven got sick again." He shoved the cart into Alex.

Alex stood there and didn't say anything.

Courtney didn't understand why he didn't defend himself.

There were a few other shoppers standing behind Van, nodding. "We don't want you here," Van's wife said.

Van walked around the cart to stand directly in front of Alex. Alex had his back against the shelves, and Courtney heard them rattle together as Van pushed Alex against them.

"Let's take this outside," Alex suggested. "It's not fair to Betty to ruin her store." He stepped to the side and started heading to the storeroom and the back door.

Betty took that moment to come running with a mop from the closet and jabbed Van in the back. When he turned around to see what was going on, Betty slipped between him and Alex. "That's enough," she said. "Alex, go."

Van took one step in his direction, but Betty wielded her broom once again and poked him in the mid-section. "Stay," she commanded.

As Van hesitated, Alex disappeared out the back door.

Courtney assumed he was running along the back path to their house. She turned to see the other shoppers staring at Betty.

Betty put down the mop and put her hands on her hips. "If you want to shop in my store, you'll be polite to all my customers." She emphasized "all." "Do not come in again if you can't be civil."

Van scowled at Courtney.

"And that includes Courtney, Van. This is your only warning. As for the rest of you, the same goes. Now get back to your shopping or get out of my store." She picked up the mop and marched back to the closet where it belonged.

Courtney heard the slam of the closet door and slipped over to an aisle devoid of customers. She wondered what Alex felt as he left. He wouldn't have liked leaving without giving Van a fight, but he knew the best thing to do for Betty and Courtney was to leave without further violence. She loved that about him.

Courtney hauled the empty boxes out to the recycling dumpster, and Betty came out the back door.

"They're all gone, dear," Betty said.

Courtney nodded and headed back into the store. "Thank you for understanding. It was nice of you to stand up for us."

"It was the right thing to do. Next time, Alex can stay in the store, and I'll make the others leave." Betty stared at her with shrewd eyes. "Besides, I know more about two years ago than you might think."

Courtney's mouth dropped open.

"Some of us aren't as thick as the rest of people around here. Why don't you go and finish up the grocery shopping your husband started and take it on home? I can manage the store until one o'clock." She smiled.

Courtney gathered her wits and smiled back. There had been many times Betty stood up for her in the last two years. She never considered Betty knew more than the rest of the community, but she was Barbara's friend, which might explain her words. "Are you sure?"

"Yes. Go on with you. I believe your young man could use your support right now, and you could use his. Go."

Courtney walked over to the other woman and gave her a quick hug. "Thank you. For everything." She started walking toward Alex's abandoned cart. "And remember, if this gets too bad around here now that Alex is out of prison, I'll quit, and you can have some peace."

Betty made a shooing motion with her hands. "Not going to happen. It will all work out."

CHAPTER 8

Alex hustled out the back door and hurried along the path back home. Then he changed his mind. He would go for a walk. Despite the freezing wind blowing, he hardly noticed. He pulled up his collar around his ears. With that and his gloves, he was comfortable enough and close enough to the house to not be concerned.

He remembered the scene in the grocery store. Was that what Courtney put up with for the past two years? He'd ask her when she got home from work. If it was, and it was going to continue, he would convince her to quit. Van was belligerent, but Alex didn't believe he was dangerous to Courtney. There might be others in town who felt the same way but *were* a danger to Courtney and Betty.

He smiled at Betty's use of the mop. She was a fearless lady. She'd bucked public opinion by hiring Courtney, and she'd stood up for them in the store. His smile disappeared. She shouldn't have to protect them.

He would have stayed and fought Van if he'd had to protect Courtney and Betty, but they hadn't needed him. By leaving, he'd de-escalated the situation. He sighed. He knew this wasn't going to be easy.

"She'll be okay."

The girl's voice came from beside him, and he stopped abruptly. When he looked down, he saw his niece, Amy. Despite his concerns, a grin spread across his face. "I never thought I'd see you again."

She shrugged and grinned back at him. She was dressed in her usual print leggings and short-sleeved shirt. "You must have needed me because here I am. Besides, I have a message for you."

"I did need to see you. You're the only one I want to see right now."

Amy came to visit him in the prison on countless occasions. He believed he was hallucinating the first few times he saw her. She had died in a car accident, so her appearance in his cell was inexplicable. He quickly got the message she was there from Heaven to help him through his incarceration.

He would never have considered a seven-year-old as someone God would send to a prison, but Amy didn't have any fear or anxiety about the situation. He gradually relaxed his vigilance when she was around, realizing no one else could see her when she visited, and God protected her.

"I have a few messages for you," Amy said.

Obviously the cold didn't affect her. Alex figured God had a warm shield around her.

"Messages?" This was different. Usually, God sent her to comfort him when he felt depressed in prison. Just having another person who wasn't threatening near him calmed him down. Plus, the knowledge God loved him enough to send her brought him closer to God.

He'd started reading the Bible, making notes in the margins and memorizing scripture. Slowly, he saw Amy less and less. Probably because he had started feeling God's presence even when Amy wasn't around.

"What messages?" Alex asked.

"The first message is that, by Christmas, everything will have changed. You're near the end of this trial."

"What trial?" Alex turned back toward home because, even if Amy wasn't cold, he was freezing.

"What you're going through now. You'll know what to do soon to get out of the situation with all the townspeople." Amy skipped along, and Alex had to stop himself from telling her she was going to slip. She wouldn't slip. Or, if she did, she wouldn't be hurt. God would see to that.

He had no idea how anything could possibly change, and her message made no sense to him. In fact, Steven didn't have long to live, and when he died, the whole community would probably band together and start their house on fire.

Amy reached for his hand and squeezed. "God got you through prison, right?"

He felt a surge of courage rush through him. He squeezed her hand in return. "Right."

"I have to give you the other message and then go because Courtney's going to be here soon to talk to you."

He never questioned her knowledge of things to come anymore. She knew things he didn't. They stood in his backyard. "Okay. What's the other message?"

"It's time to talk to Courtney about becoming a pastor or missionary." Her clear gaze met his.

"But Courtney told me we didn't have any money for me to go back to school."

"Maybe that's true, but God will find a way. You know that," she half-scolded him and put her hands on her hips in mock outrage.

"Okay." He laughed and pulled her to him in a quick hug and let her go. She was precious to him, and he hadn't gotten to know her until he was in prison.

Paul and Samantha hadn't kept in touch before he went to prison, and he had to admit, he and Courtney hadn't reached out to them often either. When Paul lost Samantha and Amy in a car accident, Alex had already been in prison for over a year. Courtney told him the news about their death on one of her visits. Then Amy started coming from Heaven to visit him, and his whole life changed once again. He still needed to tell Courtney about Amy.

"Remember what I said. Everything will work out. Bye," she said and was gone.

CHAPTER 9

Courtney hurried home from the grocery store. The bags she carried were heavy, but she only wanted to make one trip. She struggled along under their weight. By the time she got home, her nose and cheeks felt frozen.

Alex jumped up from the couch and hurried to take the bags from her. "Why didn't you call me? I would have come down and helped carry them."

"I didn't want a repeat of this morning's fun." She heard the bitter note in her voice. She was tired of the whole thing. She wanted to stay home and rest, but someone had to make money, and it wasn't going to be Alex. Not here in Chokecherry Valley anyway. No one would hire him.

His head jerked up, and he stared at her. "I'm sorry you went through that. At least I got to leave."

"Oh, Betty let me hide in the back room until everyone was gone. Then she let me check out these groceries and bring them home. I'm here until one o'clock." She dumped the last bag on the counter beside the ones he'd already placed there.

While he started unloading groceries and putting them in the fridge and cupboard, she shed her coat and boots and stifled a sigh. She didn't want to go back to work. Just looking at Alex today irritated her. She knew it wasn't his fault, but he was the closest person on whom to unleash her frustrations. She didn't want to do that.

"Why don't you rest on the couch while I whip up something for lunch?" he asked. "You must be tired."

She didn't answer right away. She was close to telling him everything she felt. She collapsed on the couch and adjusted the throw pillow beneath her head. She closed her eyes and prayed for patience. She heard Alex moving around the kitchen, cupboards opening and closing, the suck of the fridge door opening and the quiet whoosh of it sealing shut.

She started to relax. She didn't like what happened this morning. "I think we're going to have to move to Bismarck." She hadn't meant to say it out loud, but she was glad she had. All movement stopped in the kitchen, and she opened her eyes and lifted her head.

Alex stood between the island and the fridge staring at her. "Why do you say that?"

She lay back down on the pillow and put her hand over her eyes. "Alex. They hate us."

"Not everyone."

A short laugh burst from her. "Right. Not everyone. But enough."

She removed her hand from her eyes and sat up on the couch. "Sit down." She pointed to the chair across from her.

He sat and leaned toward her, his elbows on his knees. "We can get through this."

"I don't want to anymore. Today showed me things won't change. Everyone…okay, not everyone, but a lot of people feel the way Van does. I can't continue to work this way, and Betty doesn't deserve the skirmishes that will continue to break out.

"I'm tired of not knowing when someone is going to come in and start shouting at me or turning down a different aisle to avoid me. I'm tired of eggs and tomatoes thrown at the house. I'm tired of not inviting my family here because I'm afraid of what's going to happen to them if someone decides to come and demonstrate on our lawn. I'm afraid, Alex. I'm tired of being tired and afraid."

She leaned back against the couch and watched him absorb all she said. She'd never told him how she felt, but today something in her had broken. Something that couldn't be put back together the same way.

"I didn't know you felt that way. You never said."

Alex looked like she'd struck him, and she felt sorry for him. "There are a lot of things we need to discuss that neither one of us has told the other."

"You're right. I have some things I should tell you too. About prison, and about this morning," Alex said.

"I hope they're good things because I don't think I'm in the mood to deal with any more problems today." She knew that was a selfish thing to say. What was he going to tell her about prison? She'd been afraid someone would kill him or beat him up or harm him in other ways while he was there. He had certainly calmed down since he'd come home a week ago, but he was still hyperalert, and she anticipated that could take years to go away, if it ever did.

"One thing is fantastic, and the other…well, it's fantastic in its own way too. Just more complicated," Alex said.

"I'll take the one fantastic, less complicated thing, and then you go back to making lunch while I digest your information and rest," she said. "The more complicated fantastic thing can wait for another day."

He looked uneasy but got up and returned to the kitchen.

What did he have to say that he couldn't tell her while looking at her? "Alex, speak. You're driving me crazy, and we've already had a rough morning. It's fantastic, right? That means good. So…"

He started to crack the eggs he set out on the counter. "Okay. Here goes." He refused to look at her and finished with the eggs. Then he chopped scallions. "When I was in prison, I saw my niece, Amy. She would come to me and keep me company in my cell."

Courtney tried to wrap her mind around what he'd said. His dead niece visited him in prison. His dead niece. "Um…"

He finally looked at her. As he took in her expression, his own face turned grim. "You believe I went crazy."

"Well…not exactly." But what? What did it mean?

"She was real." His voice was now firm. He quit lunch preparations and watched her reaction. "I really did see her, and she did come from Heaven to visit when I needed her. When I was at my lowest points, she was there. I know you're going to say I imagined her, but I didn't. In fact, I saw her again this morning on the back path when I left the grocery store."

"You saw her again," she spoke slowly. "This morning."

She studied his expression. Who was this man? Did she know him anymore? They'd been apart for two years. "And this is your fantastic news from prison?"

"Yes." His look was steady, but he stayed where he was.

Perhaps he sensed she needed the space to take this in. She did. It would take days. A moment later she realized she was also jealous. If he saw Amy, why hadn't God sent a comforter to her? Why him? She immediately felt ashamed.

"Well, I think it's fantastic. It proves there's a God and a Heaven. I didn't grow up in the kind of family you did. You had steady parents who took you to church and taught you about God. I'm happy for you. But I guess God decided I needed to learn about Him in a different way." He went back to getting the omelets ready for lunch. "I know you need time to absorb this. I know I did."

She sat there, listening to the butter sizzling in the pan. That was why Alex's omelets tasted good. He melted butter in the pan and then poured in the egg mixture. The omelets had a wonderful buttery crust around the outside. Why was she thinking of buttery crusts when Alex just told her he'd seen Amy?

"What did she say to you this morning?" Courtney asked.

"Does that mean you believe me?" Alex's eyes searched her face.

"I don't know, but if you believe it, I'll try. It's going to take me a while."

"Okay. If or when you want to know more, just ask me. It's not a secret from you. The idea takes getting used to, I know. It took me a long time to accept it."

She nodded. "What did she say this morning?"

"She said I would know soon what to do about the situation with the townspeople."

"Move away from here," Courtney announced.

Alex thought about that for a minute before turning back to the pan on the stove. "Perhaps. One thing, we can't leave before Steven's death. They need us."

"Agree. But you will consider moving, won't you?" Courtney asked.

Alex plated the omelets and set them on the island. "Yes, I will consider it. We can talk later about plans if you want."

He took a few muffins from the counter and placed them on another plate beside their omelets. "Come eat. The rest can wait, like you said."

She was suddenly hungry. Maybe her husband had a breakdown in prison. He seemed normal now. She didn't know what to believe. She wasn't going to solve it in the next hour. She'd eat lunch and then lie down. She did need to rest.

They were quiet throughout lunch, and Alex did dishes while she lay down. She fell asleep, thinking of sweet little Amy and wondering why her own life had gotten more complicated instead of less since Alex came home.

CHAPTER 10

Courtney woke up from her nap and found herself alone. She looked at the clock and was astonished to see she'd slept solid for three hours. She'd missed work. She never missed work.

She hurried into the main part of the house to ask Alex why he hadn't woken her. There was a note on the island that said he was visiting Steven and Barbara. He called Betty, and Betty said Courtney should take the rest of the day off. He ended the note with, "I love you."

She smiled. Their intimate relationship since his release from prison had been tenuous. It almost felt like they were new roommates circling each other, trying to figure out each other's likes and dislikes. It was strange because they'd been high school sweethearts. They'd known each other for years.

Until a two-year separation forced them to see each other in new ways. She supposed it might even be good for them not to take each other for granted. When she remembered his comments about Amy, she was concerned.

Suddenly she had an idea of who could help her. She found her cell phone on the coffee table and called Ashley. Ashley was at work, so she left a message, but that was okay. She asked her to call as soon as she could.

She was surprised when the phone rang ten minutes later, and the caller identification displayed Ashley's name.

"Hi," Courtney said. "How are you able to call during the day? Aren't you at work?"

"No. My clinical observation class is finished. I'm doing last-minute prepping for a speech I need to make. It's the final one, and I'll be so happy to finish the class.

"What's up? You never call me. I figure it must be important."

Courtney laughed. She and Ashley had their moments since Alex went to prison. They forbade Ashley to visit. They meant to keep the stigma of Alex's reputation from spreading to his family.

"Well, it's a question I have for you about Alex."

"Is something wrong with him?" Ashley's concern came through loud and clear in her panicked tone.

"No. At least I don't think so." How could she ask if Alex was having a breakdown? "Alex said he saw Amy when he was in prison. He said she came from Heaven and visited to comfort him when he was depressed. I'm concerned he's had a breakdown. He said he saw her again this morning after an incident at the grocery store."

"Really?"

"Yes, but the grocery store story can wait."

"Well, I know he's not going crazy," Ashley's voice was calm now, as if they were talking about nothing more important than the weather.

"How can you be sure?" Courtney asked.

"Because there have been other people who have seen Amy too."

"Who?" Courtney demanded.

"Just a minute. My doorbell's ringing."

Courtney sat on the couch, listening to the silence for what seemed like a long time. She heard the back door opening and Alex shedding his outerwear. She didn't want him to know she called Ashley about him. At least not yet.

Finally, she heard background noise on the other end of the phone, and then Ashley's voice. "I've got to go, but everything's okay. Paul and I will be coming out to see you and Alex this evening. I promise to explain then. We'll eat before we come, so no need to go to any effort."

Then silence, which was for the best because Alex joined her in the living room. "Hi. How are you feeling?"

"Much better. I needed the rest, but I wish you hadn't called Betty. I should have gone to work."

"You needed the break. Van must have stirred up some of the other residents because Betty had more complaints this afternoon." He joined her on the couch. "I'm sorry. I should have stayed home. We should sell this house as soon as something happens to Steven. It's almost over."

Courtney pushed her own problems aside. "How was he this afternoon?"

"Really weak. He hardly spoke. I did most of the talking, and that was with Barbara. Mary was there and glared at me the whole time, until Barbara told her to go to her room until I left."

"I bet that made her mad."

"She stomped off to her bedroom, but they both laughed and said she had always been a handful. Then they reminisced about her a bit. It seemed to make them happy." Alex looked thoughtful. "I guess I'd rather she be mad at me than them, so I'll try and visit when she's not there."

"Me too," Courtney said. "I'll call before I go over there."

The next few hours were quiet. Courtney found a book to read and settled deeper onto the couch although she found herself reading the same page over and over. Alex read his Bible and made them something to eat.

Courtney told him Ashley and Paul were visiting sometime that evening, but she wasn't sure when they were coming. Alex seemed excited at the idea. She was glad they were visiting but restless at the thought of Ashley bringing up Amy.

Courtney broke the unspoken rule of keeping Alex's secret, and she hadn't wasted any time in doing it. Trust was hard to come by, and this might be a big deal to Alex. She couldn't wait for Paul and Ashley to arrive, and she could get the evening over with.

They finally arrived around 7:30 p.m., and soon all of them gathered in the living room. Everyone refused anything to drink, but Courtney got herself a bottle of water from the fridge. Her mouth was dry, and she needed something to do with her hands, or she knew she'd be twisting the wedding band on her left hand the whole time they were there.

She debated about how to bring up the subject, as everyone did the initial greetings and talked about the lack of snow. They were discussing how cold it was supposed to be in the few weeks until Christmas when she broke into the conversation.

"I called Ashley today," Courtney said to Alex, who sat beside her on the couch. He turned his head in her direction, but she avoided his gaze. She looked at Ashley, who sat in the chair across from her. "We talked about Amy."

Paul looked at Ashley and then turned back to Courtney and Alex. "What's going on? Why did you call Ashley about Amy?"

Courtney couldn't look at Alex. She took a drink from her bottle of water.

Ashley broke the silence. "Alex saw Amy while he was in prison."

Paul's gaze focused on Alex. "You did?"

"I did." Alex's gaze was steady. He didn't appear upset at all. "I guess I can forgive Courtney for calling Ashley."

He reached over and took Courtney's free hand. "I told you I was fine."

"I know you did, but you have to admit it's weird."

"Yes, it was. But it's normal now. However, I also remember how it felt in the beginning before it became normal, so I understand your concern."

Alex turned to look at Paul and Ashley. "But you don't have to be concerned. Amy was a comfort. She'd bring messages to me from God, and her being there helped me. Of course, at first I was appalled she was in a prison seeing the other prisoners, but it didn't faze her at all. When I realized I was the only one who saw her, I relaxed a little. After a while, it became natural."

"I totally understand what you're talking about," Paul said. "The same thing happened to me."

Courtney dropped her bottle of water at the shock of his words. "How come I didn't know?"

They looked at her, and she blushed. Oh. Right. They'd forbidden Ashley and Paul to contact her or Alex in the past few years. Of course they weren't going to call up just to announce something hard to understand.

She picked up the bottle of water and went to the kitchen for a towel to soak up the excess spilled onto the wood floor. Then she settled back on the couch, waiting for the story.

"First of all," Ashley said, "you're no longer alone. You have us, and Hannah and Jason. Don't forget again," she admonished but smiled too. She gestured to Paul to continue.

"After Samantha and Amy died, I was in a bad state. By that time, I'd been sober only about a year. I was trying not to drink again, but the grief was nearly intolerable. Amy started appearing at my worst moments and helped me get through those times. She helped me stay sober.

"I know it seems strange a seven-year-old helped me stay sober and helped you in prison, but that's what happened. I think she also helped Ashley's boyfriend's family. Amy seems to be sent to Earth to help those who are depressed," Paul said. "I will tell you, when I first saw her, I went to the hospital and had brain scans and saw a psychiatrist." He laughed.

"Of course, the scans showed nothing. The psychiatrist helped me to deal with things, but I kept seeing Amy. Finally, I knew she was sent from God to help me and not a figment of my imagination. After that, I accepted the situation. Since Hannah and I have become closer, I see her less often. At some point, her part in helping me will be over, and I won't see her any longer." His face softened. "I appreciate those extra times I had with her. And I'm glad she's helping you."

Alex got up and hugged him.

Courtney didn't think she'd ever seen the two brothers hug before. Not even on her and Alex's wedding day. Of course, at the time, Paul had been drinking heavily and wasn't always easy to be around.

When they'd settled back down and the conversation resumed, Alex spoke up. "I guess I don't need any medical tests."

Courtney, who listened and watched the whole scene between the guys unfold, laughed. "I guess you're okay. At least in relation to Paul."

Paul laughed. "Right. If you want to consider me normal."

"Hannah thinks you're okay," Ashley finally inserted herself into the conversation.

"Have you ever seen Amy?" Courtney asked her.

"No. But I guess I didn't need as much help as my brothers."

"Hey now," they both objected in unison.

She smirked at them.

The gathering wound down, and Paul and Ashley drove back to Bismarck, as they both had to work the next day.

Courtney had to work too. If Betty let her. Was she out of a job? How could Betty handle this busy Christmas time by herself? Everyone was buying baking ingredients and other goodies for the holidays. She'd worry about that tomorrow.

CHAPTER 11

Alex lay awake after he'd said goodnight to Courtney. She was still sleeping in the guest bedroom. He felt like he was calming down enough to have her sleep with him, but he was taking it slow. He wanted it to be right.

The whole thing with his family tonight showed him Courtney didn't totally trust his mental health. Of course, he'd had his own doubts when he'd first seen Amy in prison, but he gradually learned God had a plan. Amy was the conduit.

He recalled Paul's story of seeing Amy after she died in the accident. They'd had the same experience. He'd felt closer to Paul and Ashley tonight for the first time in years. Even before he went to prison, he hadn't felt close to Paul.

Ashley was closer to him in age, and they had been closer than Paul was with either of them. The whole dynamics of their parents dropping them all off in various places played a role. He was glad

Ashley at least had some stability while she lived with their grandmother in Bismarck.

He hadn't wanted to leave his friends in Chokecherry Valley, so he'd put up with being under the watchful eye of Steven and Barbara. Since they didn't have boys, they were pleased to be stand-in parents while his parents travelled.

Paul unraveled during that time. He'd started drinking too much and partying all the time. Strangely enough, he'd gotten away with it because his grades were always good. He'd made it through med school despite everything.

Then he'd married Samantha, and they'd both spent their evenings drinking and clubbing. Then one day, Paul had enough of the life. Alex decided something happened that woke Paul up to what they were doing to Amy. Maybe he felt like they were abandoning her the same way their parents abandoned them. Whatever happened, Paul had gotten sober.

Amy kept him sober after her death. It was an amazing story. He was glad he had his own experience with Amy, or he wouldn't have believed Paul's story. Courtney was having a hard time believing it all. He could tell from her decision to read in the guest room as soon as Paul and Ashley left.

She was probably lying awake too. As if the thought made her materialize, she was suddenly standing in the doorway.

"Can I come in?" she asked.

She must have assumed he was also awake. "Sure." He slid over to the other side of the bed and patted the empty space beside him.

She came in and sat down. "Are you mad at me?"

"Why would I be angry?"

"Because I told your family what you said. I know we should keep some secrets between us, but I was afraid for you. Ashley is taking psychology classes, and Paul is a doctor. I didn't think she'd tell Paul unless we asked her to, but then I didn't know Paul had the same experience with Amy you did. Anyway, I'm sorry."

He sat up against the headboard and stuffed the pillow behind his back. "I'm not sorry. It worked out for the best. If you hadn't called Ashley, I wouldn't have known about Paul and Amy. At least not for a while."

"You're right," he continued. "We should keep some things between us, but we've been apart for two years. You've learned to make your own decisions without consulting me on everything. That's okay." He stared up at the ceiling. "I wish there had been a different way to do things back then, but there wasn't."

She lay down beside him on the bed and cuddled close to him. "I missed you, but I'm not sorry. We did what was necessary. There's no going back."

He put his arm around her and pulled her closer. "What if you've lost your job?"

She laughed. "We'll manage somehow. We both know we might have to move to Bismarck after Christmas. It's becoming obvious this isn't possible for us to stay here."

"Well, before we leave, we'll enjoy the last bit of time we have here. If you can't work tomorrow, do you want to go with me to find a Christmas tree?"

"I'd love to. We can start decorating and put more cheer in the house," Courtney whispered.

"For me, the best cheer in the world is seeing your smile. But we'll decorate anyway."

"Also, if I can't go back to work, I'm going to bake. I feel the urge to make something. Let's invite your family here for Christmas. We'll have

Paul and Hannah, and Ashley and Jason. If Jason isn't busy with his own family."

"Sounds good to me." Alex was pleased at the idea of hosting Christmas at the house. "One last Christmas here before it's sold. Although there isn't much to compare to in the past, since our parents weren't always around for Christmas."

"Oh, well. Less to live up to on my part then." She laughed.

He loved her husky, sweet laugh. Though, he wished their situation didn't make laughing such a rare event these days.

"Amy also told me it was time to become a pastor or do missionary-type work," Alex said. He hated to fling it out into the room, but he needed to say it.

At least Courtney didn't pull away from him. "Alex, honey. We talked about it. We don't have the money."

"How much money is it going to take? Maybe there's a stipend or some kind of fund for those who want to become a pastor. We have a house to sell. That should bring in money," Alex said.

"Which we need to use for food and shelter in Bismarck while I search for another job. You know it's not going to bring in much. Rural North Dakota real estate isn't big money." She patted his arm.

"There's got to be a way. God wants me to do this. Amy even said it was time." He knew it would work out, but how was he going to convince Courtney? She didn't see Amy.

He'd known this was his path in life for over a year. He'd just told her a short time ago, and she needed time to adjust to the idea. "Let's drop it for tonight and make plans after Christmas."

He could feel her relax against him.

"Yes. Let's get through Christmas, and then make plans."

CHAPTER 12

Alex woke up to the feel of Courtney's kiss against his cheek. She started doing that soon after he'd returned home. When he told her he might hit her in his sleep without knowing it was her, she learned to kiss him and step back quickly. He admired her considerate response and enjoyed the morning wake-up.

He promised to make breakfast in the mornings, but she only wanted something cooked about half the time. The rest of the time, she ate fruit and a boiled egg. She made her own toast, because she said he didn't know how to make toast without burning it. He had laughed. The toaster was temperamental, and he got distracted instead of watching it closely to make sure it didn't get stuck in the down position. He'd even set off the fire detector one morning.

Now he got up and joined her in the kitchen where she stood by the sink. It was one of those mornings where she didn't want a cooked meal. He sat down on a stool by the island.

"I'll go see Steven this morning while you're at work, and then, when I get home, I'll start doing the decorating inside. Where are the decorations?" he asked.

"They're either in the garage or in the attic. I didn't decorate last year, so they're probably dusty." She set her cup in the sink.

"Okay. I'll shake them off outside or in the garage. If they're in there. Is there something specific you want to help decorate?"

"Just the tree. I want to go with you to choose one and decorate it together." She walked around the island to his side and gave him a quick hug.

He hugged her back. "Okay. How about we go pick out a tree in the morning after church tomorrow and then ask Paul, Hannah, and Ashley to help us decorate in the afternoon? Maybe Ashley would like Jason to come over."

"Sounds good." She had her boots and coat on and held her bag with her shoes and other things she might need. "You're not overdoing the people part? I thought you might want to spend more time without constant company."

"I'm fine. It depends on the company, and we've kept it to family and Steven's family."

"True."

He scuffed his bare foot against the floor while watching her pull her scarf a little tighter. "I have to admit I'm wondering how your family will treat me when we meet them for church tomorrow."

"There won't be any physical fights, if you're worried." She smiled wryly. "I can't promise there won't be scowls thrown your way."

"Well, I guess that's only to be expected."

"Mom and Dad will be pleasant and courteous. That's their way. They know I'll be mad at them and not visit if they aren't nice to you, so I guess we'll get through it. At least we're not going to visit their house before or after the service. We'll be in public the whole time." She opened the front door. "Try not to worry. It'll pass fast."

She was right. It shouldn't be a big deal, but he didn't want her at odds with her family. He jumped up from his stool and hurried over to the door. He just had to kiss her before she left for the day.

She leaned into his kiss, and he finally pulled back. He grinned at her, and she gave him a bemused look.

"Wow. You were holding out on me before," she said.

"I needed to know you still loved me," he said.

"And what happened this morning?"

"I know you talked to your family about me and reined them in. That was nice of you."

She left with another bemused shake of her head.

He finished his own breakfast, showered, and found the Christmas decorations in the garage. He left them in place, not wanting to get dirty before visiting Steven and Barbara. He'd move them into the house when he got home again.

He snuck across the back lane, mindful of the altercation in the grocery store the day before. Sarah opened the door when he knocked and motioned into the living room without greeting him.

Barbara sat on the chair beside the hospital bed. She held yarn and a knitting needle but wasn't knitting anything with them. There were only a few rows done, and it looked about the same as last time he visited.

Sarah sat in the recliner and picked up her book, ignoring him. Mary glared at him from where she sat in a chair across the room.

Glancing at her father, who was sleeping, she said, "You shouldn't have come."

"Mary!" Barbara's look held a warning.

"Well—"

Barbara interrupted her quietly, "If you have a problem, go into the other room for a while."

Mary sat there frowning for a few minutes longer. Eventually, she gave up and went into the other room, as they both ignored her.

Barbara and Alex carried on a quiet conversation without a lot of meaning. Steven could wake up at any time, and their talk was meant to be soothing. Alex was about ready to leave when he finally woke up. His gaze was hazy, and it took him a few minutes to orient himself.

"Hi," Alex said from the chair he sat in. He pulled one up next to Barbara.

"Alex." Steven's voice was soft and wispy. "It's good to see you."

"You too. We were talking about Christmas trees. I'm going with Courtney tomorrow to get one. The one you've got decorated there by the window is wonderful."

"Got it from Van," he whispered.

"Good plan. Courtney and I decided to get an artificial one. We'll be picking one out tomorrow," Alex said.

Steven reached out slowly.

"He wants you to take his hand," Barbara said.

Alex grasped his hand.

Steven looked him directly in the eyes and squeezed his hand. "Thank you. You've been a great friend."

Alex nodded. "You're welcome. Thank you for taking care of me when I was younger."

"Never been a better kid than you, except my kids." His eyes drifted closed.

Alex could feel tears forming and surreptitiously wiped them away. He stayed a little longer, but Steven remained asleep. Alex put his hand gently on his shoulder when he got up to leave.

Barbara trailed him to the back door. "It's almost time," she said quietly.

Alex nodded. "Want a hug?" he asked. "It's a tiny payment for all those hugs you gave me when I got hurt when I was younger." He knew this was a lot bigger hurt than any of the ones when he was young.

He gave her a big hug, and she pulled his head down to kiss him on the cheek. "You always were a good boy."

He left with more tears in his eyes and didn't bother to wipe them away. He somehow knew that this was the last time he'd be able to talk to Steven.

When he got home, Alex got out all the Christmas boxes from the garage. He needed something physical to do to keep himself busy. Nothing would take away the image of Steven in his hospital bed. As he gathered the decorations, he prayed for him and Barbara and their girls.

He opened the boxes on the far side of the living room to keep them out of the way. Courtney could help decide what she wanted to use from them. A lot of the decorations were from the Richmond family's Christmases. Ashley and Paul only took a few of the ornaments when they moved out, but he and Courtney made additions in their time together.

He started pulling out strands of garland and untwisting them. He realized what he needed to liven up the room was Christmas music. He got up and put his phone on the channel for Christmas carols.

He laid out all the garland in strips on the floor and was working on the string of lights for the tree when he heard the door open.

"Oh, wonderful," Courtney said when she saw what he'd done. "I'm excited to be celebrating Christmas with you this year."

Alex got up from the floor and walked over to give her a kiss. "Your lips and cheeks are cold."

She pushed him away slightly and unzipped her coat. "It's cold out there. You can warm me up later." She fluttered her lashes at him.

He laughed and moved away to give her room to get her boots and other outerwear off. "How about hot chocolate?"

"I'd love that."

When she finally settled on the couch, he brought her a cup of cocoa with a coaster and a snowman cut-out cookie on a plate.

"Christmas cookies? Did you bake?" She picked up the cookie, inspected the frosting and then took a huge bite. "Yummy," she said around the food in her mouth.

"Please," he objected with a grin, "no talking with food in your mouth. By the way, I can bake."

She swallowed and took a drink of her cocoa before putting the cup back on the coaster. "Perfect temperature. Sure, you can bake, but you didn't bake these."

"How do you know?" He plopped on the couch beside her.

"Because the icing is done neatly, and you slap the frosting on when you do cookies." She laughed.

"Well, there are a lot of cookies to frost. It takes forever if you are too careful where you put the icing," he said defensively.

"Which is why I know you didn't bake. The kitchen is still in one piece."

"You're right."

She finished the cookie and picked up her cup again, holding her hands around the mug. "In spite of that, I appreciate the snack."

"It should hold you over until we eat, but if not, there are more in the kitchen."

She jumped up, went over to the island, and grabbed another cookie. "I'm starving."

"We can eat earlier, if you want."

"Okay."

"How about in an hour…about five? If you get hungry this evening, you can have more cookies."

"You sound like you're talking to a toddler, promising sweets."

He shrugged. "If the shoe fits." He slid back down to the floor and started untangling light strands again.

"I'd throw a shoe at you if I still had one on. Yes," she said, "my heavy winter boot."

"Why don't you join me on the floor here instead?" Giving her a wink, he patted the floor beside him.

She swallowed the last of her cocoa and put the mug in the sink. "Good idea."

She joined him, and they companionably worked together. He heard her humming to the music and was content. For the first time since he returned, he felt like he was home.

They enjoyed an early meal and spent the rest of the evening putting up decorations and finishing the Christmas cookies Barbara sent home with him. They even watched part of a Christmas movie together, until Courtney fell asleep in his arms on the couch. He stayed awake, watching her sleep, and relishing the opportunity to hold her in his arms.

CHAPTER 13

When he awoke in the morning, he was on the couch alone and could hear the shower going in their bedroom. He had a crick in his neck from sleeping in an awkward position, but it was worth it.

For breakfast, he made a hashbrown, sausage, and egg casserole, which he stuck in the oven and went to take his own shower. Courtney had the next two days off, and yesterday must have gone okay at work. She hadn't said otherwise or looked stressed when she got home.

They enjoyed joking throughout breakfast, and then drove to Bismarck to pick up an artificial tree. Singing along to Christmas songs was the most fun he'd had since yesterday. Courtney had a lovely voice, but she didn't know the words to all the songs. What she didn't know, she made up. They laughed all the way to the store.

It didn't take them long to pick out the tree. A six-foot balsam fir. It already had fiber-optic lights. They could change the color of the lights or make them twinkle as the mood struck them once it was set up.

Courtney teased him about straightening out all the light strings and said he'd wasted his time. He shook his head at her and told her it had been relaxing.

They invited Ashley and Paul to come over in the afternoon to put up the tree and help decorate, and they agreed. Paul was bringing Hannah, whom Alex hadn't met yet. Ashley wasn't sure but mentioned Jason might join them for a short time. It all depended on the Christmas errands he had to do for his family since there were only a few weeks to finish up before Christmas.

Courtney and Alex took time to eat lunch in Bismarck and were ready to hang the rest of the strings of lights around the house when they got home. They had extra now that they didn't need them for the tree and agreed any they didn't use could be donated.

"I'd like to bake cookies before they get here. It'll make the house smell Christmassy," Courtney said.

"Sure. I'll help you with the frosting," Alex teased.

"I think not. You work on the lights. I'll do the cookies."

They were still joking with each other when their first guests arrived. Ashley, Paul, and Hannah arrived in a flurry of chilly air. When they'd all settled into the living room, Paul wandered over to the box with the tree in it. "Wow. Top of the line, man."

"You bet. We're going to put this up for years to come. It needed to be a sturdy tree," Courtney said before Alex could get a word in.

"It even has those cool fiber-optic lights," Hannah said. "I tried to talk Paul into them, but he insisted on the old-fashioned ones."

Alex was glad she was comfortable joining in the conversation. She looked like she'd fit right into the family. Of course, he'd only met her ten minutes ago, but Paul looked content in her company, even in the short amount of time Alex observed them.

"Old-fashioned is fine." Paul tapped her on the shoulder. "They still light up."

"But you don't have the option to change colors on the tree every few seconds," she teased him.

"Oh, ours has this lovely switch," Courtney said. "You can have several colors at once, or only white ones, or only blue ones, or—"

"We get the idea," Paul said dryly as Hannah sent him a triumphant look.

Ashley asked for a knife to open the box. "Let's get this thing up."

Courtney went into the kitchen to get one for her.

"Is Jason coming over?" Alex asked her.

"Yes, but he has babysitting duty. Chloe doesn't need much. She's only five months and will play happily with her toys on the floor. She's not quite crawling yet, so we're probably safe for this Christmas. Next year, she'll be getting into everything."

"Who is Chloe?" Courtney handed Ashley the knife.

Ashley took it and started slicing the tape holding the box together. "She's Jason's niece. His sister lives with him and his parents. She had a rough time with postpartum depression, but she's better now. She's finishing up her G.E.D. and is going to surprise her parents with her diploma on Christmas Day."

"Terrific," Courtney said, helping pull the box open.

Soon there were two big pieces of tree they'd pulled out of the box. Alex and Paul took over because they were taller, and easily plugged the two pieces together. Once they stuck the trunk into its holder, everyone started fluffing the branches.

As they started to decorate, Jason showed up with Chloe. They all took a break to coo over her. Then Jason laid her on her blanket in the middle of the living room with her toys, and they started decorating the tree.

Alex turned on the Christmas music, keeping the volume lower than earlier in the day when he and Courtney had belted out the songs on their drive to Bismarck. He smiled at the memory.

"You look happy," Paul said quietly beside him.

"I am. I feel like I'm finally home. It took a while."

Paul bumped Alex's shoulder with his own. "Sometimes things take time."

"Good things," he agreed.

They didn't say any more. The women were more vocal as they hung ornaments, and Alex enjoyed listening to them talk. Since he'd been away, he felt like this was a way to catch up on some of the community happenings and people.

They hung the last ornaments and took all the empty boxes out to the garage. They stood around admiring the tree and the garland and lights hanging on the door frames. Alex set a few gold and red candles at various places around the room, and there was a nativity scene set up on a table in the corner.

Then they all collapsed on the chairs and couch and sighed as one.

"That was fun," Courtney said. "Thank you all for the help. This was a great idea."

"I believe it was your idea," Ashley teased her.

"Right. I will take credit," Courtney agreed.

Alex punched Paul lightly on the arm as he headed into the kitchen. "I got a prize when I married her."

"Don't you forget it," Courtney called across the room.

Ashley joined him in the kitchen. "What can I help you with?"

"You can see what everyone wants to drink. We have water, soda, or apple cider. Or I can make hot cocoa. I'm feeling hot from all that work, so it's not likely anybody will be interested."

"Sure. I'll ask."

While Ashley started divvying up drinks, Alex got the cookies and a plate of fancy cheeses together. Then he pulled out paper plates and napkins and lined them all up on the island. "Snacks are served. Help yourself."

Ashley didn't even wait to sit down before starting to munch on one of the cookies. "Yum. Ginger cookies. My favorite. No one makes these anymore, but I could smell ginger when I walked in here today. I was hoping I was right."

"Courtney made those just for you. She remembered you liked them," Alex told her.

"I love them, and they're fresh. Amazing, Courtney."

"Thank you," Courtney said.

Alex thought she looked almost shy as she took the compliment. He decided he better get on the ball and praise her more often. Underneath her tough exterior, she had a soft heart. He should know, after what she'd gone through to stick with him.

When their company left, Courtney and Alex settled back on the couch together. It became their favorite place to cuddle.

"You did a great job hostessing today," he told her.

"So did you." She turned sideways to face him. "You seemed happier today."

"Well, we had a great time going to pick out a tree, didn't we?" Alex hoped she'd agree. He knew he'd had fun, and she appeared too also.

"I did. You have a horrible voice." She poked his stomach.

"I know. I usually don't sing very loud. I try to let others drown me out. Except today. I was having too much fun."

"Trying to be louder than me, but not on key." She laughed and tucked her arm in his. "Remember tomorrow when we're at church to sing quietly."

"I will." He wasn't looking forward to seeing her family tomorrow morning. His family accepted him and Courtney since he'd gotten home, but he wasn't expecting the same grace from Courtney's family.

He knew Courtney warned them to behave, but he would still feel the weight of their thinly

veiled displeasure. He had tonight to enjoy the
evening before facing them, and he put thoughts of
them aside.

CHAPTER 14

Courtney's family treated Alex about like he'd expected when he arrived with her at the church. A few ignored him. A few said a muted hello. Her parents politely continued with small talk. Frowns abounded when they thought their parents and Courtney weren't watching them.

Two of her brothers and two sisters joined them. Her other sibling attended his own church. Alex sat at the end of the pew with Courtney between him and her family. She sang along with the songs, and he sang quietly so only she could hear. He caught her glance at him once during a song, and they smiled.

Attending church again was the one bright spot of the morning. He was glad Courtney refused to join her family for lunch after church. She told them that, after Christmas, they would consider visiting them. He didn't know what else she told them, but they accepted her word.

The following weekend, she was going to join her family on a shopping spree for Christmas, and they were going to have an early get-together at her parents' house. He hadn't decided if he would join Courtney yet or not, so they kept the option open.

When Alex and Courtney got home from church, they stopped at Steven and Barbara's house. They entered the living room together. Mary and Sarah sat there talking quietly.

The girls stopped whispering while Barbara talked briefly to Courtney and Alex.

There was a sudden hush in the room as Steven took a deep breath and let it out. They all looked at him. He was no longer breathing. Alex could tell instantly.

So could the family. Mary took one look at her dad and then looked over at Alex. "You killed him. It's all your fault." She rushed at him with her hands out as if to shove him, tears pouring from her eyes.

Alex held his hands in front of him, palms out. "I'm sorry, Mary."

"You're not sorry. You got what you wanted." She sniffled.

"Enough," Barbara said, taking Mary's arm and pulling her away gently. "Girls, we have to talk." She gave him a meaningful look.

He knew what that meant, and Courtney did too. They both said goodbye to Steven by touching him on the shoulder. Then they said goodbye to Barbara and left through the back door.

"She's going to tell them about their father, isn't she?" Courtney asked.

"Maybe." Alex didn't like what this would mean for the family, but Barbara hadn't totally agreed with Steven on this subject. He likely knew, when he died, she would tell the girls the truth.

"Sad," Courtney said.

"Very."

"Is there anything we can do?" Courtney asked.

"Probably not. The neighbors will be stopping by constantly now with food and condolences, and we're not welcome. It would make it harder for Barbara. She knows she can call if she needs us." He wished they could do more, but there was nothing to do.

He knew the vigil and funeral were already planned, and Barbara just had to go through the motions. And grieve. Unfortunately, there was no help for grief, except time.

CHAPTER 15

Courtney showed up for work as usual the Monday after Steven's death. There were a lot of customers, and she was glad she'd been assigned to work. They picked up ingredients to make food for the Hanson family and for Christmas. Christmas was the following week on Friday, and there wasn't much time left for those wanting to bake.

She overheard people talking about lighting candles and standing outside Steven and Barbara's house singing hymns. The weather would be frigid that evening. The temperature dipped to the single digits, and snow was forecast for the next day.

She knew from Betty, the vigil would be tomorrow, and she and Alex talked about whether they should attend. Alex thought it would be best to steer clear, considering many of the townspeople believed his actions at the bank made Steven sicker. Most of them reasoned he treated Alex like a son, and Alex betrayed that trust.

Alex refused to tell anyone the truth. Courtney knew she and Alex did the right thing, and they weren't going to the vigil. It would make it easier for Barbara and the girls. She and Alex said their goodbyes yesterday. Steven was in Heaven now and knew how they felt.

While she restocked shelves, she considered Alex's dream to help people. She knew he was meant to follow that path, but she still didn't see the way they could make it work. She needed to pray more about it. She'd been concentrating on praying Alex would be okay in prison and been relieved when he returned safely home.

He changed, but she still loved him. They were returning to the closeness they'd had before he left. They might even be getting closer than before. Despite everything, there seemed to be an additional level of intimacy in their relationship.

That was probably due to Alex's new relationship with God. She sighed, realizing suddenly that meant she had to help Alex make his dream come true. She'd been fighting the idea. Now, she knew why.

She liked to know Alex was safe at home. She didn't want him to go out into the world and be unsafe again. Why hadn't she realized the reason for her reluctance sooner? Because she was still adjusting to everything. Getting out of Chokecherry Valley was of paramount importance to their continued survival. They'd never get out from under the cloud of Alex going to prison.

After helping Betty, she returned home that afternoon. The day continued to be busy, up until her exit from the store. She'd asked if Betty wanted her to work later, but Betty waved her away. She stressed that Courtney should keep supporting her young man. Courtney smiled at the old-fashioned term and at Betty. She couldn't have asked for a better boss.

Betty knew she couldn't wait to leave the store every day since Alex got home. Yes, she wanted to be with Alex, but she also felt the tension when one of the townspeople spent their time in the store scowling at her. Courtney was thankful the people in town stayed kind to Betty.

She got home to find Alex sitting on the couch reading his Bible. She smelled something good cooking in the oven. "What are we eating this evening?"

"Pot roast, baked potatoes, and apple pie for dessert." Alex laid his Bible on the coffee table and got up.

"Yum. I need comfort food after today." She'd removed her outdoor wear and joined him by the coffee table. After a quick kiss, she sat down on the couch, and he sat beside her.

"Was it a difficult day?" Alex asked her.

"Busy. Everyone's getting ready for the holiday. Of course, there were also the shoppers for hams and casseroles and everything else people will take to Barbara." She laid her head on the back of the couch and closed her eyes.

"The Hansons' attorney called and wants us to be at the vigil tomorrow."

She jerked upright and turned to look at his face. "Are you serious?"

"Do I look serious? I wouldn't joke about that."

Although he'd been restless since he'd gotten home, he'd never used a sharp tone with her. She understood his view though. She felt the same reluctance about going to the vigil he did.

"I'm sorry." She took his hand, leaned back against the couch again and pulled him over to her. "Come cuddle."

He promptly slid next to her, but his frown remained. "I don't like this. Just because Steven wanted us to be there. We loved each other. He was a second father to me, and I believe he felt like I was a son.”

“He wants you to know his feelings. He wants you to have the same opportunity as everyone else. The ability to say goodbye.”

“But he knows we said goodbye at his house.”

“Maybe he told Bob to call you before you were even out of prison,” Courtney suggested.

“Bob said he just talked to him a few days ago and stressed I should be at the vigil.

Courtney sighed. “I guess we’ve been through worse things. That sounds terrible. I didn’t mean I don’t want to go to the vigil to support Barbara. But Mary and Sarah aren’t going to like it. We’re a reminder to them now.”

“I know, but I guess we’re stuck because I also got a call from Barbara asking me to come. It was one of Steven’s last wishes.” He groaned. “I can’t wait to move out of here in the new year.”

“I agree,” Courtney said. “I guess this is a good time to tell you something good. I was thinking about your dream to become a pastor or do missionary work. I was hesitant to let you do it.” She laughed as she sat up and grabbed his hand.

“What about it?” he asked, surprised.

"You're a grown man."

He smiled into her eyes. "Yes, I am."

"But I feared losing you. When you start helping people, you're not mine anymore. You belong to everyone in the community. And you belong to God. You aren't mine anyway." She brushed her hand along his cheek. "But I realized something else."

"What's that?" he asked.

She noticed his smile was gone, and there were tears in his eyes. This meant a lot to him, and she hadn't understood until today. He had come home, only to still feel alone. She thought she was helping by shielding him, but she wasn't helping at all. Thank goodness he had God to see him through.

"I realized you already belong to God. I realized you're meant to do work for Him on Earth. I realized I love you and want you to have what you want in life to be happy. Since you've been chosen by God, and that's what you want to do, then we'll find a way to work it out. I'm sorry I didn't understand the importance sooner."

He pulled her into a big hug. "What did I ever do to deserve you? I can never repay you for all the things you've put up with since marrying me."

She couldn't see his face, as her own face was buried in his soft sweater, but that didn't matter. They would be okay together. "No repayment. We're one in the sight of God. You are a remarkable man, Alex Richmond. God recognized it sooner than I did. Of course, He had the advantage of making you."

CHAPTER 16

Alex didn't want to be at the funeral home for the vigil. Bob Fuller, Steven's attorney, convinced him to attend the service. He would have stayed away if Barbara hadn't also asked him to be there.

He sat in the back row, along with Courtney. Paul and Hannah brought Ashley from Bismarck to be there, and Jason arrived with his family. Everyone in the small community knew Steven, and that included Jason's family. They were seated right in front of Alex's family.

Alex couldn't help but be aware of the hostile looks thrown his way. He'd overheard more than one person asking why he was allowed to stay. He tried to sink into the seat, but there was no hiding his presence.

He saw Steven's brother, Parker, talking to the funeral director, and the funeral director looked Alex's way. They weren't standing far from where

Alex sat, and he heard Parker tell the funeral director to have him removed.

The funeral director headed in his direction when Bob intercepted him.

"Alex stays," Bob said. "It was one of Steven's final wishes. I'm sure you don't want to go against that." He put his hand on the brother's shoulder. "Alex doesn't want to stir anyone up. He's going to sit there quietly. I'm guessing he doesn't want to be here either, but I asked him to come, and he did."

Parker grudgingly nodded and sat down without looking in Alex's direction again.

"I don't understand what's going on," Courtney whispered in his ear. "Why would Steven put you through this?"

Alex shrugged. "We were friends. He knew I wanted to be here to say goodbye."

Courtney leaned back in her chair.

On her other side, Paul patted her shoulder. "Hang in there. This is going to get more interesting."

Courtney swiveled to look at him. "More interesting? I want peace."

"Soon. You'll get it soon. You're right. This is all unusual, and I believe a plan was put into action."

Soon the doors at the back of the room were closed, and the pastor stepped up to the podium to begin the service. He started out with a prayer for Steven's soul. After he stepped down, Parker read a Bible passage, and then Mary read a verse from Psalms. The funeral director stepped up to the podium.

"Before we get to the part where everyone shares any memories or prayers for Steven, we have a special request. Steven called me a few days before his death, and I stopped by to visit with him. He wrote a letter when he knew he was dying. He asked his close friend and attorney, Bob Fuller, to read this letter to us now."

"No!" Alex shouted and stood up. "It's not necessary."

Bob was already standing behind the podium. He looked at Alex with sympathy. "It's what he wanted."

To Alex's surprise, Barbara stood up from where she sat in the front row and joined Bob. "It's time."

"It isn't necessary," Alex said to Barbara.

"I appreciate your position, Alex, but it's time," Barbara repeated.

Mary and Sarah went to stand beside their mother and nodded at Alex. He had no choice but to sit down. They weren't going to stop.

Courtney whispered to him, "What's he going to say?"

"Listen," Alex responded, his eyes focused on Bob. He clenched his hands into fists. Steven hadn't needed to do this. Tears stung his eyes. He felt Courtney rubbing his back, trying to comfort him.

Bob adjusted the microphone at the podium and started reading.

Dear Friends and Family.

Thank you for being here for my family. I'm honored you took the time to come. I've appreciated your trust in me and all the times you have been there for my family and me. Serving you as bank president was a dream come true. During my time at the bank, I hope I helped you navigate your financial futures in a wise way. I tried my best.

At this point, if I were standing in front of you as I should be, I'd be clearing my throat. Because what I have to say next is not what you would expect and does not reflect well on me or my character. In fact, I have been a coward not to tell you this information sooner. Before my death. To leave this world and ask my good friend Bob to read this is dishonorable.

I apologize to all of you. And I apologize to my daughters, who were unaware of the true circumstances of everything that happened two years ago. There is no hiding from you now. Or from God's judgment. May He have mercy on my soul.

My wife urged me to tell you at once. I hope, as soon as you know the truth, you won't treat her badly.

Two years ago, money was stolen from the bank. That is common knowledge to this community. What isn't known is I took the money. Alex did not. Alex has been blameless in this entire situation. He tried to put the money back into the bank to save me from prosecution. I was going through my first chemo treatment and was short of money. I figured I'd take the money, pay for treatment, and then, with my next paycheck, return the money.

It didn't work that way. There was an audit, and Alex tried to cover for me so I could spend more time with my family. We did not know the outcome of the cancer treatment at that time, so when the auditor saw Alex tried to put the money back, he assumed Alex had taken it in the first place.

He didn't. I did. I'm begging for your forgiveness now for my family. As I said before, I have been a coward. They don't deserve to suffer for my actions, and my daughters were unaware of what I did. Every time Barbara tried to talk me into confessing, I refused to listen.

This next part will sound like an excuse, but it's just an explanation. There is no excuse for what I did. When I went into remission, I was going to confess. But I didn't. Then the cancer came back, worse than ever, and I knew this was the end.

Alex told me many times he was fine with the way things worked out. He told me prison wasn't that bad. I'm sure it was a lie. Courtney also paid the price by being away from Alex, and by being a pariah in the community. She handled it gracefully and said she agreed with Alex. They both deserve your respect for letting me spend my final years at home with my family, and for upending their lives for that to happen.

Now it's time for the truth to come out. Alex didn't do anything wrong. I did.

I apologize now, when it's too late for me to allow you the chance to tell me face-to-face what you think of me now you know the truth.

My desire is you will treat Alex and Courtney with the respect they deserve for their great sacrifice. I never had two better friends than them.

Thank you, Alex and Courtney, for putting your life on hold. I plan for this letter to be used by my attorney, Bob Fuller, to have your record cleared. Bob holds a further letter with full details for the courts.

I want to clarify two things. Bob never knew the truth. Alex and Courtney were unaware I would ever reveal the truth.

There's really no way to end this letter, except with an additional apology to you all. I hope you remember the good times and forgive me for my greatest failing.

May Christ's Peace envelop you all.
Steve

CHAPTER 17

There was a long hush when Bob finished reading the letter. He moved back from the podium and sat down again in the front row of chairs.

Barbara stepped up to the microphone. "I'm sorry."

As tears fell down Barbara's cheeks, her daughters led her back to their chairs. Sarah and Mary looked shocked at the news that had been unleashed on the mourners.

Alex tried to control his own tears. He felt Paul's warm hand on his shoulder. When he felt more under control, he stood up. He didn't look at anyone, but he could feel their eyes on him as he walked down the aisle toward the front of the chapel.

Courtney suddenly jumped up to walk beside him. Always with him. He took her hand, which was as sweaty as his.

He stopped and stood in front of the microphone, Courtney beside him. He started talking directly to Barbara. "Your husband was a fine man. I loved him like a father. When my siblings and I were growing up, we had little support. The whole town knows how my parents liked to travel without their children. Steven and you were and *are* my family." He looked at Mary and Sarah and smiled. "And Mary and Sarah are two extra sisters for me."

He looked out at the congregation. "You may be feeling cheated and let down by Steven right now. I've never felt that way. He made a mistake at a time when he was sick and desperate. Who among us hasn't made a mistake in our lives?

"Some of our mistakes have been small, and some have been big. But even the small mistakes have ripples. Ripples we may never understand on Earth. I know when you all have time to process this news, you will remember the good things about him and forgive him for his mistake. I pray you will treat Barbara and her family with respect."

He looked at Courtney. "We did what we could to give Steven time with his family. He had so little of it left. We were happy to help ease some of his misery." He smiled at Courtney, and she smiled back.

He stepped away from the podium, touched Barbara on her shoulder as he walked by her, and walked back down the aisle and out of the building.

His family quickly joined him outside. Paul gave him and Courtney their coats and hugged each of them. Hannah took her turn with hugs, and Ashley followed her example.

"Let's talk when we get back to the house," Paul suggested.

They had all come together, squeezing into one car. They walked to the car in silence and drove back to Alex and Courtney's house.

When they'd all gotten their winter outerwear put away, they trooped into the living room and dropped into their respective places on the couch and chairs. Alex looked around at his family.

Ashley was curled up on one end of the couch beside Courtney, who sat beside him. Hannah and Paul each took seats on the stuffed chairs across from them. The only one missing was Jason, who attended the vigil with his family and stayed with them.

"Well," Paul said. "That was quite a shock." But he didn't sound surprised at all.

"I'll say." Ashley nudged Courtney. "Why didn't you two tell us?"

Alex shrugged. What could he say? He and his siblings drifted apart by that time. Paul was drinking. Ashley moved to go to college. He and Courtney felt it best not to put the burden of keeping the secret on anyone else.

"Does Courtney's family know?" Paul asked.

"No. The only people who knew were me, Courtney, Steven, and Barbara. Their daughters didn't know until last night. Barbara told them yesterday because she had a feeling it was going to come out somehow. Maybe Steven warned her. I didn't know he was going to have his confession read at the vigil."

"It will change your life, you know," Ashley said.

She sounded so adult to Alex, who still thought of her as younger. She only had one week of school left to earn her four-year degree although the graduation ceremony happened in the spring.

"I know. But the change will be gradual. There will always be people who won't believe what Steven wrote. And people who will be mad at them because we did keep this secret. But I don't care. If Courtney and I are good, I'm good." He put his arm around her shoulders and leaned back on the couch. He took a big breath and let it out.

"It does feel good to not have a big secret weighing on me anymore. Especially with all of you. You're my family, and I know we haven't been as close as some families. However, I did miss you while I was in prison. I made the promise to myself, when I got out, I'd develop a relationship with you all if you were interested." He smiled.

"Am I jumping to conclusions that's what you want too?" He looked from Ashley to Paul and Hannah.

Paul got up and clapped him on the shoulder. "Even without the truth, I was ready to accept you." He turned to look at Courtney. "You too. You're my sister."

Ashley and Hannah each got up and took their turns hugging him and Courtney.

"I know we've hardly even spoken yet," Hannah said. "But I'm claiming sister status with you all right now." She hugged Alex too.

Ashley headed to the kitchen. "This calls for refreshments."

Courtney jumped up and joined her, and Hannah followed. Alex and Paul moved to stools at the island, watching the women search through the cupboards and fridge.

Courtney said to Ashley, "You were seriously a pain in the neck. Coming into my kitchen, like you did my house a month ago."

Ashley smiled at her. "That's what sisters do."

Alex could tell the two of them had made peace and were trying to lighten the mood.

They were soon all eating cheese and crackers, washing them down with soda and water. They talked a bit about Christmas, and all of them agreed to come back and celebrate Christmas with Courtney and Alex at their house. The good mood gradually turned somber.

"Are you going to the funeral tomorrow?" Paul asked Courtney and Alex.

Alex replied, "I hadn't intended to go. I didn't want to go tonight either, but Barbara and Bob convinced us to go. Now I know why. Barbara would be fine either way. I'm not sure what's best. If we go, there will be a lot of staring, which I'm used to, but that detracts from the reason we're all there. But if we're there, we can support Barbara. I don't know what the best thing to do is."

"Go," Courtney and Ashley said in unison, then looked at each other and laughed.

"We'll go to honor Steven," Courtney said.

Ashley nodded. "It's about him. It's like you said at the vigil. He was a mentor to you. You deserve to say goodbye, like everyone else. I don't think anyone will say anything to you or to Barbara about the embezzlement. They may look, but that's all."

Paul nodded. "I agree. If you want to go, I'll go with you."

"Me too," Ashley said.

"I guess we're all going."

The gathering broke up, and Hannah and Paul took Ashley back to Bismarck.

CHAPTER 18

After locking the front door behind their guests, Courtney and Alex wandered back to their favorite spot on the couch to cuddle.

"Well," Courtney said.

"Yeah," Alex agreed, "this changes a lot of things."

"Does it?" Courtney asked.

He looked at her in surprise. "Of course. Now we can stay here in Chokecherry Valley. Once everyone is used to the idea I didn't embezzle any money, they'll start treating you normally again."

She shook her head. "I don't want that to stay here. Besides, if you're going to help the neighborhood wherever we settle, we both need to get good jobs. That way we can pay for your college courses."

"I can probably find a job around here now." Alex wasn't sure what he'd do. People might be willing to hire him, but what kind of jobs were available in a small town like Chokecherry Valley and the surrounding area? He'd have to at least travel some miles to get a decent job. People around here didn't have much to pay an employee.

"Do you want to stay? I mean really, Alex. Do you want to stay here in this house, or would you rather move? We have a chance to make a fresh start anyplace if you want." Courtney's voice was reflective.

He couldn't tell if she wanted to move or stay. "What do you want? You're half of this team. I can take a lot of online classes. If you want to stay here in Chokecherry Valley, then we can stay. We'll figure out the money later. It's been an emotional day, and it's late."

She sat there quietly snuggled up to him for a while. Finally, she said, "You're right. It's late. I don't know what I want right now. It's been a crazy day. Let's sleep on this and consider things for a few days."

"Good idea," he said. "We agreed we weren't doing anything before Christmas anyway." He lifted her chin and looked into her eyes. He felt close to her tonight. It was time. "Do you want to stay with me all night?"

Her eyes lit up her whole face, and a wonderful smile curved her soft mouth. "I'd like that. I've been waiting for you to feel comfortable at home."

"I'm home with you. It's going to be okay." He believed it now. The unbearable secret they'd been carrying for two years was finally off their shoulders. The relief surprised him. He thought he had come to terms with living with the lie the rest of his life. He'd learned lies were toxic.

CHAPTER 19

The funeral was sad, but there were no outbursts from anyone. A few people shook Alex's and Courtney's hands and apologized. Some still avoided their gaze. Probably embarrassed. They'd come to terms with the new status quo eventually.

The flurry of the week before Christmas continued at the store when Courtney was at work. Alex saw a new light in her eyes when she got home and knew she was feeling the same relief he was that the truth of the embezzlement was known.

Steven's attorney called and was trying to get Alex's case reversed, but Alex didn't care. Yes, it might help with his reputation, but he didn't feel it would make any huge difference in his life.

His biggest relief was Courtney's family knew the truth. They surrounded her with love while he was in prison, but he knew she had to deal with their wrong assumptions about him. She'd been hurt but was willing to hide the truth. He was glad she didn't have to worry about their judgment any longer.

Christmas day drew nearer, and he and Courtney hadn't discussed whether they would move or not. He gave it a lot of thought and leaned toward moving. He briefly considered he'd be helpful to Barbara by staying, but she informed him her sister lived in Virginia, and she was moving there as soon as the girls graduated from college.

Could he sell their family home? His parents had lived here, and his grandparents in their time. Would he be the one to sell it? When he bought it from his siblings, he assumed he'd live the rest of his life in the town. Things changed. God changed him. His path in life would never be without unknowns. He'd learned that lesson.

Although he felt led to help others, he was uncertain of his abilities. He kept reminding himself he would have God to lead him through it all. And God gave him Courtney to help him. He couldn't doubt that after what she'd been through and still stuck with him.

His greatest joy was that she had started asking him questions about God. It showed him she was serious about deepening her own faith.

He decided he'd done enough sitting around for the day and took a walk to see Barbara. A few other women were there when he arrived, and they greeted him cordially.

Barbara's sister from Virginia was staying with her. Barbara's daughters were also with her now until the New Year because school was over for the semester.

After checking if she needed anything, he left, reassured she had the help she needed. He would leave it up to her as to when she wanted to talk to him again.

He did his usual cooking after baking more things on the list Courtney wanted to serve for Christmas. Then he went online and started researching the process to become a pastor. The information he found showed it would be a lengthy process.

Courtney was right. They were going to have to earn some money first. He would contact the church liaison to begin the process of acceptance into a program, but classes would have to wait. In the meantime, he could help in whatever community they decided to live in.

In the middle of eating that evening, Courtney put down her fork and announced she'd made a decision. They were sitting in their favorite spot in the bay window at the table in the kitchen.

"We should move. Your family is in Bismarck. My family is spread around the state, but my parents are in Bismarck too. I don't want to work at the grocery store any longer. Betty won't need me when the holidays are over anyway."

Alex gazed at her across the table. "That's a good idea. I second everything you've said."

The relief on her face was obvious. She jumped up and kissed him, and then sat down again on the bench with a blush on her cheeks. Her eyes glowed brightly. "Good. Because there's something else I've never told you."

He looked at his vibrant wife, who suddenly appeared more alive than he'd ever seen her, except on their wedding day.

"I've always wanted to start a retreat center. A place for people to go to reset when life has dealt them a blow. A sanctuary for people who have lost loved ones, or are making a big decision, or," she paused. "Well, anything where a person needs a break for about a week."

She held up her hand to stop him before he could speak. "I know. It'll take money."

He got up and joined her on the bench in front of the bay window. "We'll find the money somewhere. It's an absolutely wonderful idea. Let's do it. I'll be helping you, which is helping other people. It's exactly what we both want to do. Becoming a pastor is a long process anyway, and you'll have my help for a long time before we need to make any other decisions."

They were ready for a new life.

CHAPTER 20

Alex and Courtney joined her parents at their church in Bismarck for Christmas Mass. The evening service was beautiful with the church decorated in bright red and green. The nativity scene at the altar had been repainted this year, and everything gleamed with newness.

At least Alex felt that way. It was like he'd been living in a bleak desert and had finally come out into the light of a green oasis. He knew he and Courtney had a long road ahead of them, but in his heart, he was already settled.

Courtney's family greeted him enthusiastically, and all of them individually pulled him aside to apologize. Her parents had come out to Chokecherry Valley a few days ago to express their regret over their behavior and talked to them about the whole situation.

He'd been happy to tell them there were no hard feelings. He did what he had to do by taking the blame for Steven and hadn't expected anyone to accept that with equanimity.

He loved the new glow on Courtney's face as she finally felt accepted by her family again. Since they made the decision to move and follow their dreams, she had been happy and lighthearted.

This Christmas felt like the best Christmas he'd ever had. He felt closer to his own siblings than ever before. He felt purpose in his future with Courtney as they worked together to build a retreat center. Courtney's acceptance of his dreams and God's call were miracles.

After church, they returned home and started the meal. They worked well together in the kitchen. Alex set out candy and cookies on the coffee table and the other decorated table they'd set up in the living room for Christmas.

Hannah and Paul arrived first. Ashley and Jason soon followed. Jason said he could stay until after the meal, and then he was going to join his family with Ashley. They all gave Ashley a hard time about leaving them.

She blushed and laughed at them. Alex could tell Jason made her happy.

After that, the day was one laugh after another. They talked over each other often.

After they'd eaten the big meal of turkey and all the fixings and desserts they could handle, Paul held up his hand to get everyone's attention. "Hey, guys," he yelled.

They were finally quiet.

"Hannah and I have something to say." Paul and Hannah were seated on the couch together, where Alex and Courtney usually cuddled at night. Paul took Hannah's hand, and she held it out to show everyone the bright ring on her finger. "We've finally chosen a date."

Courtney and Ashley screamed and jumped up to hug Hannah. "Congratulations!"

Alex and Jason chimed in their congratulations, and Alex hugged the happy couple too. Jason settled for smiling at them both.

"When's the wedding?" Ashley asked.

The happy couple looked at each other. "Next year in May. We're keeping the wedding small. Friends and immediate family."

"That's wonderful," Alex said. "As long as we're sharing news, Courtney and I have news to share too."

"We're selling the house and moving. We're looking around western North Dakota for a larger place." Courtney explained their plans, and there were more congratulations and offers of help.

Courtney's eyes glowed happily. "I'd love any help we can get."

There was more hugging, and then Jason and Ashley had to leave. Hannah planned to stop at her sister's house also. They left shortly after Jason and Ashley.

Courtney looked at Alex when they were gone. "That went well."

"Definitely. No one even questioned us selling this house."

"Were you worried about it?" Courtney asked.

Alex considered it. "I didn't think so, but the relief when no one brought it up was a comfort, so I guess I was."

They soon found themselves settled on their favorite seat on the couch.

"Merry Christmas." Alex brought a small box out of his pocket and handed it to her.

She took it from him in surprise. "We weren't giving each other gifts this year. We agreed being together was gift enough."

"We did, but I couldn't resist." He smiled as she fumbled with the wrapping paper.

When she opened it, she found a small, exquisite gold angel on a chain. She looked up at him with awe and a huge smile. "It's gorgeous."

"So are you. She reminds me of you. My angel." He kissed her.

~~~

Check Out The New Series Featuring Courtney and Alex
Crocus Hill Inn Mystery Series
Picture of Book 1 – The Last Owners

~~~

Missing persons and half a million dollars in jewelry…
When Courtney purchases a quaint house in the countryside, her dreams of transforming it into a cozy, inviting inn appear within reach. But beneath the charming exterior lurks a tangle of dark secrets. The previous owners vanished without a trace— eight years ago.

Driven by curiosity and a sense of justice, Courtney and her husband Alex team up with Gary, the son of the missing couple, to unravel the mystery. The clock is ticking. The promise of treasure draws fortune hunters to dig up the tranquil backyard.

When a fresh murder shatters the peace, Courtney realizes that the truth might be buried even deeper than she feared. As the stakes rise and the body count grows, Courtney must decide how much she's willing to risk to bring the truth to light—and whether some dreams are worth dying for.

A traditional, twisty, mysterious whodunit set in southwestern North Dakota…

https://www.jeanrezab.com

COPYRIGHT

Cover design by Sunset Rose Books

ABOUT THE AUTHOR

Jean Rezab writes from her home in North Dakota. Having grown up on a farm, she enjoys all things country, especially wildflowers, wheat fields, and winding lanes.

She likes to entertain her readers with everything she writes. Since reading has always been a means of escape, she enlivens stories with complex relationships, sweeping her readers into other worlds. She writes intriguing mysteries and women's fiction with messages of love and forgiveness.